If he ha...
he woul...
candidate list and continue his search
elsewhere.

There was a very good chance that he would have to do exactly that.

But not yet.

No, sir, he wasn't beaten yet. Something different, and possibly very important, had happened when he'd held Amy in his arms and kissed her, and he had every intention of discovering what it was.

So, okay, Amy had an attitude and outlook so far from wifehood and motherhood, it was a crime. But attitudes and outlooks could be changed....

Dear Reader,

May is a time of roses, romance...and Silhouette Special Edition! Spring is in full bloom, and love is in the air for all to enjoy. And our lineup for this month reflects the wonder of spring. Our THAT SPECIAL WOMAN! title, *Husband by the Hour,* is a delightful spin-off of Susan Mallery's HOMETOWN HEARTBREAKERS series. It's the story of a lady cop finding her family... as well as discovering true love! And Joan Elliott Pickart continues her FAMILY MEN series this month with the frolicking *Texas Dawn*—the tale of a spirited career girl and a traditional Texas cowboy.

Not to be missed is Tracy Sinclair's warm and tender *Please Take Care of Willie.* This book is the conclusion to Tracy's CUPID'S LITTLE HELPERS series about matchmaking kids. And speaking of kids... *The Lady and the Sheriff* is Sharon De Vita's latest heartwarming installment of her SILVER CREEK COUNTY miniseries. This story features Louie, the kid who won readers' hearts!

May is also the month that celebrates Mother's Day. Cheryl Reavis has written a story that is sure to delight readers. Her FAMILY BLESSINGS series continues with *Mother To Be.* This story is about what happens when an irresistible force meets an immovable object...and deep, abiding love results.

Finally, we round off the month by welcoming historical author Barbara Benedict to Silhouette Special Edition. She makes her contemporary debut with the lighthearted *Rings, Roses...and Romance.*

I hope you have a wonderful month of May!

Sincerely,

Tara Gavin,
Senior Editor

Please address questions and book requests to:
Silhouette Reader Service
U.S.: 3010 Walden Ave., P.O. Box 1325, Buffalo, NY 14269
Canadian: P.O. Box 609, Fort Erie, Ont. L2A 5X3

JOAN ELLIOTT PICKART

TEXAS DAWN

Published by Silhouette Books
America's Publisher of Contemporary Romance

For my mother, Olive Elliott,
and her
six granddaughters

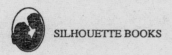 SILHOUETTE BOOKS

ISBN 0-373-24100-3

TEXAS DAWN

This edition published by arrangement with Harlequin Books S.A.

® and TM are trademarks of Harlequin Books S.A., used under license.
Trademarks indicated with ® are registered in the United States Patent
and Trademark Office, the Canadian Trade Marks Office and in other
countries.

Printed in U.S.A.

JOAN ELLIOTT PICKART

is the author of over seventy novels. When she isn't writing, she enjoys watching football, knitting, reading, gardening and attending craft shows on the town square. Joan has three all-grown-up daughters and a fantastic little grandson. In September of 1995, Joan traveled to China to adopt her fourth daughter, three-month-old Autumn. Joan and Autumn have settled into their cozy cottage in a charming small town in the high pine country of Arizona.

Welcome to Texas,
home of perpetual matchmaker Granny Bee...and her latest project:
the Bishop Boys, confirmed bachelors turned...

FAMILY MEN

Margaret Madison m.?
TEXAS BABY
Special Edition
Winter 1997
That's My Baby!

Bram m.?
TEXAS GLORY
Desire
Summer 1997

Blue m. Amy Madison
TEXAS DAWN
Special Edition #1100, 5/97

Tux m. Nancy Shatner
TEXAS MOON
Desire #1051, 2/97
Man of the Month

LEGEND:

———— The Bishop brothers and respective wives

- - - - Maternal relationship between Margaret and daughter Amy

Prologue

"My stars, look who's come back to visit their Granny Bee. I'm mighty glad to see you, I truly am.

"You bring yourself right on in here out of that rain, and sit by the nice fire I got goin' in the hearth. Help yourself to some of the hot cider in the pitcher there. I put a dab of honey from my precious bees in it to make it special.

"Tell you a story? Well, I'll just sit here rockin' in my old chair and do exactly that...tell you a story.

"What's that? Oh, you want to hear more 'bout the Bishop boys? Well, I did sort of hint the last time you came to call that things were 'bout to change in Blue Bishop's life.

"Well, now you remember that all three of the

Bishop brothers, Tux and the twins, Blue and Bram, were wantin' to get themselves married and have a slew of babies.

"What they hadn't figured on was that findin' a wife would be hard, considerin' women had been flocking after 'em like ducks to bread crumbs for years.

"Tux and Nancy, as you remember, after a lot of fussin' and fumin', up and got married. Oh, heavenly days, they are doin' fine, just so happy they seem to glow.

"Jana-John and Abe, the Bishop boys' mama and papa, are pleased as all get-out 'bout Tux and Nancy.

"Now, 'fore I go any further here with spinnin' my tale 'bout what happened to Blue, I need to be tellin' you some 'bout Amy Madison. She's one of those reporter people for that big, important newspaper folks read with their mornin' coffee. You know, the *Houston Holler* paper.

"Well, Amy's got her mind firmly fixed on bein' one of the best reporters in the state of Texas. That's the only thing that matters a hoot to her, that job of hers...now and in the future to come. She doesn't take time for another thing, it seems.

"No time at all..."

Chapter One

"I don't have time for this," Amy Madison said, smacking the steering wheel of her ancient compact car. "You...will...start," she said, narrowing her eyes.

Turning the key in the ignition again, she cringed at the ominous grinding noise, then sighed with relief when the engine caught, chugging in an erratic rhythm.

Pressing slowly on the gas pedal, Amy gripped the steering wheel tightly as the car lurched away from the curb. A quick glance in the rearview mirror revealed black smoke billowing from the tailpipe.

"This car," she muttered, "is *not* environmentally correct."

Twenty tense minutes of driving later, Amy parked in the employee's lot at the rear of the tall building housing the *Houston Holler* daily newspaper.

She hurried across the pavement, entered the building and greeted the security guard seated behind a desk in the lobby without breaking her quick stride.

The elevator carried her to the fifth floor, and moments later she entered a huge, extremely noisy room. People were scurrying back and forth, others worked at computers perched on side-by-side desks, telephones were ringing and voices created a high-volume cacophony.

Amy went directly to her desk, oblivious to the noise. Settled onto her chair, she flipped on the computer, removed a disk from her large purse and inserted it in the proper slot in the machine.

She acknowledged several greetings of "Good morning, Amy" with a waggle of fingers, then began to read the material that had appeared on the computer screen.

"Amy?" a voice said.

"Hmm?" she responded, still studying the screen.

"Gib wants to see you right away."

Amy's head snapped up, and she frowned at the young man standing next to her desk.

"Now?"

"Yep. He told me to watch for you and tell you to come to his office as soon as you got here. Our editor has spoken."

"Drat," Amy said. "Okay, I'm on my way."

She pressed several buttons on the keyboard, leaving the machine on but the screen blank, before walking away from her desk. She stopped long enough to straighten her fluffy yellow sweater over the waistband of her brown slacks, then continued across the crowded room.

Gibson McKinley's office was in the center of the area, and was constructed of floor-to-ceiling glass. Blinds had been installed to afford privacy if desired, but the vast majority of time the editor could view any section of the newsroom that he wished.

Gibson was, in actuality, the owner of the newspaper. After his wife had been killed in an automobile accident seven years before, he'd left the "ivory tower" of executive offices on the tenth floor of the building and returned to "the trenches," the ongoing madness of producing a daily newspaper, in the role of editor.

For the past five years, Gibson McKinley had been voted one of Houston's Top Ten Eligible Bachelors, a list he reluctantly allowed to be published in the *Holler*.

At forty-nine, Gibson was ruggedly handsome, with black hair graying distinguishingly at the temples. He was tall, well-built, and kept himself in shape by engaging in a variety of sports. Charming and extremely wealthy, he was seen at various society events with a never-ending number of different women.

He had no intention, he'd once been quoted as

saying, of ever remarrying, or of becoming involved
in a serious relationship.

Amy knocked on the wood framework of the office door and was waved in by Gibson, who was
seated behind a cluttered desk, speaking into a telephone tucked between his head and shoulder.

When Amy closed the door behind her, the noise
beyond was dimmed instantly to a low hum. Gibson
pointed to one of the chairs in front of his desk, and
Amy sank onto it. She crossed her legs and drummed
her fingers impatiently on the arms of the chair, her
thoughts focused on the material she'd been reading
on her computer screen.

"Sure thing," Gibson said into the receiver. "I
understand your position."

He rolled his eyes heavenward as the voice in his
ear droned on. Tuning out the dissertation he was
being subjected to, he looked at Amy.

Amy Madison, he mused, never failed to remind
him of his daughter, Betsy. They were both in their
midtwenties, had short, curly black hair, big brown
eyes, and stood about five feet four inches tall, with
delicate bone structure. Both Amy and his baby girl
were very pretty women.

But the physical similarities were the only things
linking the pair. His daughter was a smiling, happy,
easygoing mother of two, who was content to stay
home, raise her babies and have dinner on the table
at six o'clock for her attorney husband.

Amy Madison, on the other hand, was career ori-

ented...big time. She did a hell of a fine job for him,
was an excellent reporter of special features, but she
definitely had tunnel vision about her work.

The rumor mill in the newsroom buzzed that every
guy on the staff who had asked Amy for a date had
been turned down flat, with Amy saying that she had
no time at the present for social activities.

"Great talking to you," Gibson said, wrapping up
the conversation. "Yep, you, too. Bye."

He replaced the receiver quickly, then began to
roll up the sleeves of his white dress shirt, exposing
muscled, tanned forearms covered in a smattering of
black hair.

"Advertisers," he said, shaking his head. "They
think they own the paper because they buy space in
the *Holler*. That guy doesn't want his pet-food-and-
accessories ad too close to one for baby clothes in
the special Christmas sales supplement. He said people will concentrate on babies before puppies, or
whatever. Man, oh man, advertisers drive me totally
nuts."

"You wanted to see me, Gib?" Amy said, using
the shortened version of his name that he'd instructed
his staff to feel free to call him.

"Yep," Gib said. "Want some coffee?"

"No, thank you. What's up?"

"Relax, Amy," he said, getting to his feet. "*I*
want some coffee. So, have you finished your Christmas shopping yet?"

"No, I haven't even started it. Gib, I don't have

time to relax. I need to start polishing my story on my week at the veterinarian's."

Gibson nodded. He poured himself a mug of steaming coffee from a pot on a hot plate sitting on a small table in the corner of the semisoundproofed, glass-box office.

Returning to his desk, Gib sat down, leaned back in the butter-soft leather chair and took a sip of the hot drink before he spoke again.

"I wanted to speak to you about your column, Amy," he began. "The favorable response to A Week In The Life Of..." nearly doubled in the last month.

"A Week In The Life Of A High-School Principal was *very* well received by the general public. You opened a lot of eyes about what is actually going on in the school arena. Nice work."

"Thank you, Gib," Amy said, smiling. "It was an exhausting week, that's for sure. But I'm fine now. Spending the day with a vet is very calm compared to the high-school stint." She laughed. "It was a good thing all those animals belonged to someone. I wanted to take them all home."

Gibson smiled, revealing straight white teeth, and producing crinkling lines by his dark eyes. The smile softened his rough-hewn features, making him appear younger and more approachable.

In the next moment, his smile faded and he moved forward to set the mug on the desk. Propping his elbows on the arms of the chair, he made a steeple of his long fingers.

"Your column is hot right now, Amy," he said, "and I want to cash in on that fact. It's gimmicky, will run its course and that will be that. But while it's helping to sell papers, I want to step things up. I want more than one column a month from you."

Amy frowned. "That's not really possible, Gib. You know how I produce that column. I decide on the subject, *thoroughly* research it, investigate the choices I have of who I want to zero in on for my week, do the seven days, gather my notes into order, then write the column. Any way you look at it, it takes a month."

Gib shook his head. "Not anymore. No offense, Amy, but you spend too much time doing research. You can gather your data while you're living the week in the pocket of the person you're connected with.

"You said yourself that when you interviewed the taxidermist, the guy followed to the letter the procedures you'd already researched."

"How would I have been able to know if he was any good at his profession," Amy said, her voice rising slightly, "if I hadn't done my homework ahead of time? He received a great endorsement by being the subject of my column. I had to know he was top-notch in his field."

"True," Gib said, "but don't forget that he already had a wall covered with certificates. Your research wasted time. He was an expert. You certainly knew that going in.''

''But—''

''I want two feature columns a month of A Week In The Life Of.... Not one, but two. No more discussion, and no arguments.'' Gibson grinned. ''Want to swear at me? Throw something?''

Amy glowered. ''Don't tempt me. Have you ever heard the term *comfort zone,* Gib? *My* comfort zone is to be fully prepared, every detail covered, before I move forward. That's how I produce my best work.

''Doing research my way has provided me with my comfort zone. And don't forget you've received *outstanding* articles from me over the past months after each of my weeks in the field.''

Gib chuckled. ''*Outstanding,* you say?''

''Yes,'' Amy retorted, folding her arms beneath her breasts. ''Bordering on brilliant.''

''I see,'' he said, laughing. ''Well, you definitely believe in your own talent.''

''Yes, I do,'' Amy said, no hint of a smile on her face. ''How can I expect anyone else to if I don't?''

''Good point,'' Gibson said, serious again. ''Amy, I fully agree that you've given me dynamite material with this series. The credit all goes to you. However, I'm sticking my editor fingers in your pie. Two columns a month, starting right now.''

Amy rose to her feet and gestured wildly. ''How can I do 'starting right now'? I haven't even thought about the next column. I still have to polish the vet's story.''

''Polish it today.''

''It takes me longer than a day,'' she said, sinking back onto the chair.

Gib sighed. ''Amy, give me a break here. I don't want to bark orders at you. But the bottom line is, we're going to do this my way.

''You've got to be more flexible when you work for a daily paper. I don't think you have a handle on that yet. You were with that small weekly for two years, which gave you the luxury of fine-tuning everything you wrote to the maximum.

''In the year you've been at the *Holler,* you've spent eight months doing A Week In The Life Of... column. Well, the party's over. It's reality-check time.''

The telephone rang shrilly, and Gib snatched up the receiver.

''McKinley,'' he said.

Amy turned her thoughts inward, ignoring Gib's side of the telephone conversation.

Darn that Gibson McKinley, she fumed. He'd just pulled the rug out from under her. How did he expect her to produce her best writing for publication if he didn't give her enough time? As the owner and editor of the *Houston Holler,* didn't Gib want excellence on every page of his newspaper? One would surely assume so.

Okay, she grudgingly admitted, it had been continually stressed during her classes in college that a journalist who chose to work for a large daily paper would have to learn to write very quickly, making his or her original draft the best it could be on the first shot.

She'd had eight months of doing things *her* way, starting with having her column idea accepted and put into motion. Eight glorious months.

This was reality-check time? Well, reality was *not* making her a happy-camper reporter.

Quit pouting, Amy, she admonished herself. She was very fortunate to have a position on the staff of the *Holler,* to be working for a brilliant editor like Gibson McKinley. She was very young and very lucky to have such a plum job. She knew that—she really did.

Gib replaced the receiver with a thud, bringing Amy from her rambling thoughts.

"I'm due at a meeting," he said. "Here's the deal. I have some friends...Jana-John and Abe Bishop. We've known each other for years.

"Anyway, their son Blue owns a ranch outside of town. Jana-John got Blue to agree to have you stay at his ranch. Beginning at nine o'clock tomorrow morning, you'll be at the Rocking B to do A Week In The Life Of A Texas Rancher.

"Blue Bishop will be expecting you. He's not married, so I don't know what kind of meals you'll be served or what shape the house might be in. Any questions?"

Amy's eyes widened. "I...I don't know anything about ranching."

"You will after a week at Blue Bishop's place," Gib said, getting to his feet. "You need to actually stay there, like you did during the firefighter story, because ranching isn't a nine-to-five job.

"Maybe you should try writing the story as you go, instead of just making notes. I don't know, whatever works for you. Once you speed things up, you'll have plenty of time for two columns a month *and* a life beyond this newspaper.

"Well, that's it. I'll be looking forward to reading the column you submit about life on a ranch. I'll draw you a map later today, showing you how to get to the Rocking B."

Amy got to her feet slowly, appearing rather dazed.

"A ranch?" she said, starting toward the door. Gib followed her. "Horses? Cows? Pigs? Oh, dear heaven."

"You'll do fine," Gib said, reaching around her to open the door. "You know, I think I'll introduce you to my daughter, Betsy, one of these days. Maybe you could learn to lighten up a bit if you were around someone your own age, who is laid-back and happy, like my sunshine girl."

"Sure. Whatever," Amy said absently, leaving the office. "Chickens? Ducks? Oh, Lord, bugs. I bet there are bugs on a ranch outside of the city. Huge bugs. Enormous bugs."

"Bye, Amy," Gib said, trying desperately not to burst into laughter. "Hey, you're going to have a wonderful week. The Bishops are all good people. At this very moment, Blue Bishop is probably smiling at the prospect of having your company for a week."

Blue Bishop was *not* smiling.

He slammed the back door as he left the house, then started toward the barn. His stride was long, his steps heavy, punctuating his frustration. Reaching up, he tugged his Stetson low, producing the age-old cowboy message that he didn't wish to be approached.

Hell, he fumed. Why was it that neither he nor his two brothers could ever say no to their sweet little mother when she asked them to do something?

They were grown men, after all. Tux, Blue and Bram Bishop didn't allow anyone to shove them around, manipulate them or get them to agree to something they wanted no part of.

Except when the request came from their mother, Jana-John Bishop.

Blue sighed as he continued his trek to the barn.

Their mother was a great lady, and they loved her. The same admiration held true for their father. Neither of their parents was demanding, or interfered in their sons' lives.

Usually.

But Jana-John had telephoned him and announced

straight out that she needed a favor from her darling Blue. She'd had a request from Gib McKinley, the owner and editor of the *Houston Holler*. Surely Blue remembered meeting Gib a few years ago at a party? He was an old and dear friend of hers and Abe's and...

"Yeah, yeah," Blue muttered, cutting off the memory.

There was no sense in replaying the whole conversation in his mind. The end result wouldn't change. He was well and truly stuck with some dingdong newspaper reporter named Amy something-or-other, who would be dogging his heels for a solid week. Seven lousy days.

A week in the life of a Texas rancher? Who gave a rip? If a person was all fired up to know what was required to run a ranch, they'd own a ranch, for Pete's sake.

"Hey, boss," a voice yelled, snapping Blue to attention.

"What!" he hollered.

"Whew. Nice mood."

A short, wiry man in his early sixties appeared in the opening of the barn. He had white hair and a neatly trimmed white beard.

"What is it, Chaps?" Blue said, glowering.

The older man grinned. "You sure got a burr under your saddle this morning."

"Yeah, well, when I tell you who Amy something-or-other is, and why she's coming to the Rocking B, you won't be smiling, either. Believe me, you *definitely* won't be smiling.''

At four o'clock that afternoon, a very attractive woman in her late thirties stopped at Amy's desk.

"Amy Madison," she said, "I don't think you've smiled once today, not when I was looking anyway. What's your problem?"

"Reality," Amy said, not taking her eyes from the computer screen. "A Gibson McKinley, giant-size dose of reality."

"Ah, I see," the woman said, nodding. "I know what kind of reality *I'd* like to engage in with our Gib, but that's only going to happen in my deliciously naughty dreams, drat it."

Amy glanced up at the woman and smiled.

"You're terrible, Sue Ann," Amy said, laughing. "You're lusting in your head, or heart, or whatever."

"And in a few other places in my voluptuous body. What can I say? Gibson McKinley is a very sexy man. So," she began in a more sincere tone, "what did our fearless leader dish out to you in his reality serving to make you so gloomy all day?"

In a rush of words, Amy related what had taken place in Gib's office that morning.

"I'm still fine-tuning my week-with-the-vet column," Amy said in frustration. "Look at the time. I've *got* to do at least *some* research about ranches, ranching, being a cowboy, the whole nine yards. I don't want to come across as a total idiot when I meet that Blue Bishop guy. Ohhh, I'm so stressed I could just scream.''

Sue Ann shrugged. ''Go ahead. In this zoo, no one would notice if a piercing scream was added to the bedlam.'' She paused. ''I hate to say this, Amy, but Gib is right. You need to lighten up, write your column, let it go, move on to the next one. *And* I thoroughly agree that you should start having a life beyond this newspaper.''

''Oh, this is great, just dandy.'' Amy punched three buttons in succession on the keyboard. ''Gib is acting like a father, and now you're parroting him like a mother.'' Her finger hovered over a computer key. ''Well, here goes. Print. No, wait. I think the part about the—''

Sue Ann leaned over and pressed the key.

''Sue Ann!'' Amy yelled.

''Printed. Done. Submitted for publication,'' Sue Ann said decisively. ''Come on, Amy, let's go have an early dinner before the work crowds hit and gobble up the happy-hour yummies.''

''I can't,'' Amy said. ''I'm going to the library to look up information on ranching. Sue Ann, do you think there are bugs—I mean really big bugs—on a ranch?''

''Probably. And big horses. And big cows. And big, strong, strapping cowboys in tight jeans and sexy Stetsons. Oh, mercy, I do adore cowboys.''

Amy laughed and shook her head. ''You're absolutely hopeless.''

"No, I'm a healthy woman, who has a nice balance of work and play. I do my society column, then forget it when I walk out of here. C'mon, let's go eat. You can't do research on an empty stomach, and I know you didn't leave your desk for lunch. Up. Now. We're gone."

Amy turned off the computer and got to her feet.

"I want to stop at the print terminal," she said, "and take a quick look at my column in hard copy. I've never submitted off of the computer screen before. I do a final read of the printout. You know, nip and tuck, polish, spit-shine."

"Not this time," Sue Ann ordered. "You've been given a direct command from Gibson McKinley to speed it up and turn in two columns a month. You have to retrain your brain."

"But—"

"The first order of business is to *feed* your brain." Sue Ann paused. "*Blue* Bishop? Now, *there's* a terrific name for a cowboy, if I ever heard one. Do me a favor and call me from that ranch of his to tell me if he does wonderful things for a pair of jeans."

"Oh, good grief," Amy said, rolling her eyes. "I can't handle this reality Gib dumped on me."

"You're stuck with it," Sue Ann said, "so smile."

Chapter Two

Amy yawned, blinked several times, then told herself to concentrate on driving.

She was so tired, so terribly sleepy. She'd stayed up until nearly two-thirty in the morning, studying dry, dull material on ranching.

She glanced at the passenger seat, knowing the canvas tote bag perched there was filled with books from the library, each boring volume dotted with scraps of paper that marked places bearing information she thought she might possibly need.

Another yawn erupted, and Amy ended it with a deep frown.

She hated, *really hated,* feeling so unprepared, so frazzled, so unorganized. She would arrive at the

Rocking B with facts on ranching floating around in her foggy brain like scattered, dry leaves blown by the wind on an autumn day.

Somehow, she decided, she was going to fake it, give the ever-famous Blue Bishop the impression that she was there to gather *further* data on the week in the life of a Texas rancher, to add to her already-vast knowledge.

"Right," she said dryly. "I'll knock him smack off his cowboy-boot-clad feet with how much I know about his dumb ranch."

Bugs, Amy reminded herself suddenly, actually shivering. She should have checked out a book about Texas bugs, so she could be on alert for the creepy-crawlers that might be, at that very moment, waiting to attack her.

She was terrified of bugs. It was just one of those fluky personality things, she supposed. Some people detested broccoli. Amy Madison hated bugs.

Amy's attention was caught by a Sold placard attached to a Realtor's For Sale sign, which was stuck in the dirt on the side of the road.

"Hope you folks like bugs," she muttered to the unknown new owners of the ranch she was passing.

She glanced quickly at the map Gibson McKinley had drawn for her. After checking her mileage, she slowed, hoping to the heavens that the sudden decrease in speed would not result in the car stopping dead as a post in the road.

The temperamental vehicle did not adapt well to

changes. It sometimes halted in its tracks if Amy was rude enough to do something as drastic as going around a corner.

Amy leaned forward, peering through the dusty windshield.

"The Rocking B," she said aloud, reading the iron scrollwork on an archway above a dirt road.

She turned the steering wheel, and the car chugged its way toward the large, two-story, pale-blue-with-white-trim house in the distance.

Blue narrowed his eyes and glowered as he saw the billow of dust approaching. He planted his hands on his thighs and pushed himself to his feet from where he had been sitting on the front-porch steps of the house. A moment later, he heard the sound of a laboring car engine, then saw the vehicle making the noise.

Was this the flashy, big-city reporter? he thought, yanking his Stetson low on his forehead. Yeah, right. Ms. Madison drove a heap of junk. Either Gib McKinley didn't pay his employees worth a darn, or Amy Madison was very, *very* low on the reporter totem pole.

Blue walked slowly to the end of the short sidewalk leading to the house, folded his arms over his chest and waited, his dark glare firmly in place.

Amy pressed on the brake, then twisted the key in the ignition to Off. The car sputtered, rumbled, shuddered, then finally stilled.

''Thank you very much,'' she said, patting the steering wheel.

As she began to reach over for the tote bag, the dust settled enough for her to see a man standing at the edge of the sidewalk.

A man she hadn't realized was there as she'd driven toward the house.

A man who appeared angry enough to spit nails.

A man who was, without the slightest doubt, one of the most gorgeous male specimens she had ever seen.

Even with his Stetson resting low, his rugged, tanned features were visible, as well as the thick black hair brushing his collar.

But it was his eyes that were pinning her in place inside her wear-weary car.

If this was Blue Bishop, his name fit him perfectly, she mused. He had the most incredible sapphire blue eyes she'd ever seen.

Blue Bishop. He was tall, had shoulders a mile wide and a broad chest. His muscled arms were crossed defiantly, stretching the fabric of his tan Western shirt, and his powerful legs were outlined to perfection in faded jeans.

Blue Bishop was a classic. His image could be used by the chamber of commerce to depict a typical Texas cowboy.

Blue Bishop did for jeans the wonderful things Sue

Ann had instructed Amy to call and tell her every
detail about.

Amy was jarred from her hazy thoughts when the
man strode forward and opened the car door.

"Are you going to sit in there all day?" he said
gruffly.

"Well, no, of course not, I—"

"I assume you're Amy Madison from the *Houston
Holler.* I'm Blue Bishop, the owner of the Rocking B. You're here for a week, whether I like it or
not. But make certain you understand this, Ms. Madison...*don't get in my way.*"

Just what she needed, Amy thought, feeling the
fury bubbling inside her, a man who was grumpy,
and rude, and blew the slogan Texas Friendly into
oblivion.

She scrambled out of the car, tilted her head back
to meet Blue's stormy gaze with one of her own and
planted her hands on her hips.

"Good morning, Mr. Bishop," she said tightly.
"Thank you for the ever-so-warm welcome to your
farm."

"Ranch," Blue shot back. "Don't ever call a
Texas ranch a farm, Ms. Madison."

"Farm, ranch," she said, flipping one hand breezily in the air. "They both have horses, cows, pigs,
dust. And bugs. Big bugs."

"Cattle, not cows. I have one milk cow. The rest
are cattle. Do you want me to spell that for you?"

Blue pulled off his Stetson, dragged one hand

through his thick, dark hair, then settled the Stetson back onto his head.

Amy watched, mesmerized by the very male action and the unobstructed view of Blue's handsome-beyond-belief face. Her mind went completely blank as she continued to stare up at Blue Bishop.

Hell, Blue thought, and damn it, too. He was acting like a jerk. It wasn't Amy Madison's fault he'd allowed himself to be roped into this asinine situation.

Amy. Pretty name. Pretty woman. She was more cute than beautiful, with a refreshing, wholesome appearance. If she was wearing any makeup, he sure couldn't tell, and he liked her fluffy, dark curls.

Her eyes were big and brown, like those of a deer—no, a fawn, because she looked young and tiny, making him feel much bigger than he actually was.

She was wearing white tennis shoes, jeans and a lightweight red sweater, that accentuated her womanly curves. Yeah, Amy Madison was a nice little package of femininity.

And she was probably ready to slug him with her pint-size fist for being so nasty to her. He owed Ms. Madison an apology. Damn.

"Ms. Madison," Blue said, then cleared his throat. "Amy. Look, I'm sorry I jumped on your case, okay? I've been waiting for you to arrive, and thinking about what I *should* be doing instead of sitting on my...porch steps.

"In all honesty, I believe that your being here to write a column on the week in the life of a Texas rancher is ridiculous. No offense meant, but it's dumb. Why don't we just call this whole fiasco off?"

Amy continued to stare at him, a rather bemused expression on her face.

"Amy?"

She blinked. "What? Oh!"

"Do you agree with my suggestion?" Blue asked. "We'll call it quits before you start this nonsense? There are probably dozens of people in other professions who would be tickled pink to have you do a story on them. It's free advertising.

"Hey, I know. I'll send you over to my brother Bram's work site. You can do a week in the life of an owner of a construction company. Okay?"

Amy frowned. "No."

"Why not?"

"Mr. Bishop...Blue, allow me to explain something to you. I usually pick my own subjects for my column. However, my editor, Gibson McKinley, has suggested that I increase my column from one a month to two, due to its ever-increasing popularity.

"Therefore, to set his proposed plan into motion, he contacted your mother, his friend, who then called you and—" she shrugged "—here we are. Gib felt he was being helpful, you see."

Blue nodded. "McKinley told you how it was going to be, and you didn't get to vote."

"I didn't say that!"

"You didn't have to. The guy owns the newspaper. I doubt seriously that he 'suggested' anything. Try 'direct order.'"

"Well, I—"

"Never mind. I get the picture."

Blue stared up at the sky for a moment.

Amy looked at the fascinating sight of his strong, tanned neck.

"Okay," he went on, meeting her gaze again, "here's a new idea. The chores on a ranch don't vary that much from day to day. So just follow me around for a couple of days and you'll have the whole story. There's really no need for you to stay an entire week."

"Why don't you want me here?" Amy said, cocking her head slightly to one side.

"It's nothing personal."

Blue smiled.

Amy's heart danced a funny little jig.

"You're an extremely attractive woman. I'd be a crazy man not to want you to visit my ranch, spend time with me and—"

"Cut to the chase," she said, frowning.

"Right." Blue's smile disappeared. "A working cattle ranch runs smoothly when everyone knows what they have to do, then simply does it. To have a greenhorn glued to me, asking questions, getting in the way, is going to gum up the program. Get it?"

"I have no intention of getting in your way, Mr. Bishop," Amy said, lifting her chin. "I've been doing this column for over eight months, and I haven't had one complaint about being a nuisance of any kind. Let's just accept the fact that I'm here for a week and get on with it, shall we?''

Two days maximum, Blue thought. Amy would have enough data in two days. McKinley would be happy, his mother would be happy, *he* would be happy. Two days, and Amy would be gone.

The problem was, how could he convince Ms. Madison that two days on the Rocking B was plenty?

Then it struck him. There was a hell of a lot more to ranching than sipping coffee beneath a mulberry tree in the glow of a picture-perfect Texas dawn. There was, for example, the mode of transportation most commonly used on the Rocking B. A horse.

Brilliant.

With what he had in mind, he might very well be able to forget two days. Amy Madison would hightail it back to Houston within twenty-four hours.

''Well, you win,'' Blue said, flashing another dazzling smile. ''Let's get you settled into one of the bedrooms, then we'll hit the trail.''

''Hit the trail?''

''Ranch jargon. Your suitcase, ma'am?''

Amy turned and opened both side doors of the car. Blue pulled a suitcase from the back seat and the tote bag from the front. He frowned at the zippered canvas bag before tucking it tightly under his arm above the suitcase dangling from his hand.

"What have you got in this tote bag?" he asked. "Bricks?"

"No, of course not," Amy said, not looking at him. "It's tools of my trade, so to speak." She leaned into the car and retrieved her purse and a laptop computer.

"Whoa," Blue said, pushing his Stetson up with his free thumb. "I've seen those things advertised. That's top-of-the-line equipment."

Blue Bishop was top-of-the-line equipment, Amy mused. That oh-so-male gesture of shoving his hat back had sent a frisson of heat slithering down her spine.

She *must* get a grip on herself. She had never before overreacted to blatant male sensuality like some teenager, and she wasn't going to continue acting out of character for the likes of Blue Bishop.

"It's imperative that I have a computer of quality," she said, "in order to facilitate the proper execution of my chosen career."

Blue chuckled. "I think they said that in the commercial I saw for those computers." He swept his gaze over her car. "Don't you consider your vehicle important? How can you be sure you can cover a story if you can't be certain you'll even get there?"

"My budget only stretches so far," Amy said. "The computer had first priority."

"Whatever," Blue said with a shrug. "For a rancher, a vehicle can be as important as his horse, depending on the circumstances. There can't be any doubt that a horse, car or truck will get you where you need to go.''

"Wait," Amy said.

She tucked the small computer under one arm, then rummaged in her large purse, producing a handheld recorder. She pressed a button on the device, nodded in satisfaction as it hummed into action, then held it up toward Blue.

"Would you repeat that, please?" she said.

"Huh?"

"You know, repeat what you just said about a rancher needing to be able to count on his horse, or vehicle, at all times."

Blue grinned. "You just said it."

"Oh." Amy snapped off the recorder and stuffed it back into her purse. "So I did."

"Hey, let's get moving," Blue said, glancing up at the sun. "I'm losing an entire morning's worth of work here."

He turned and started up the sidewalk leading to the house. Amy was right behind him, stealing a quick glance at Blue Bishop's *very* nice tush as she followed him into the house.

"I'll give you a tour of the place later," Blue said, going down a hallway.

"Yes, fine, thank you," Amy said, nearly trotting to keep up with Blue's long-legged stride.

They entered a bedroom that had been decorated with a Southwestern motif. There was a spread on the double bed in a multicolored Native American pattern, and a woven rug with similar colors hung on one of the walls. The dresser, desk and easy chair were dark wood, solid and very masculine appearing.

Blue set Amy's suitcase and tote bag on the bed, then looked at her.

"This room has its own connecting bath," he said. "I already put some towels in there. There are hangers in the closet and clean sheets on the bed. Settle in or wander around the house if you want to. I'll be back to get you in about an hour."

"Oh, I don't need that much time."

"No problem. Don't rush." Blue touched his fingertips to the edge of his Stetson, then hurried from the room.

"But I..." Amy stated, then stopped speaking and sighed.

She sank onto the edge of the bed, indulged herself in a loud yawn, then stared into space.

So far, she thought, her A Week In The Life Of A Texas Rancher assignment was *not* going well. She'd started off feeling frazzled, due to the lack of proper and extensive research, and it had been downhill ever since.

Blue Bishop obviously didn't want her around, which was in direct contrast to the reception she was accustomed when she began a week with a new subject.

Also off kilter was her adolescent reaction to Blue. It was a miracle she hadn't started drooling on his shirtfront.

Enough was enough, she told herself, rising to her feet. She was, as of that moment, getting her act together.

First of all, she would ignore the fact that she was in dire need of a long nap, though she would like nothing better than to just curl up on the bed and make up the lost hours of sleep from the past night.

Next on her agenda was to solemnly swear to herself that her childish behavior around Blue would not be repeated.

Well, no, it wasn't childish. It was extremely *womanly*. She'd felt the heat churning within her, knew it had been desire, for mercy's sake. She was a professional, a top-notch journalist on assignment. Blue wasn't a man; he was the subject matter of a column. Period.

A half an hour later, Amy had hung up some clothes, put others in dresser drawers, assembled her toiletries in the bathroom and combed her hair. The tote bag filled with library books was under the bed within easy reach.

She wandered back down the hall and entered the large living room.

Again, the furnishings shouted that a man lived in the house, as there was not one feminine touch to be seen among the heavy, dark furniture.

There was no clutter in the room, although a fine film of dust lay on the furniture. The dark brown carpeting showed the track marks of a recent vacuuming.

Despite the all-male aura, the room was attractive, the fireplace edged by flagstone definitely an eye-catcher, but Amy felt overwhelmed, as though she'd shrunk in size.

She moved on, peering into the family room, which had a more lived-in look, with magazines and newspapers scattered on a coffee table, a mug and plate on an end table.

The area boasted another fireplace, a couch and chairs, television set, stereo system and...

"A piano?" she said, walking toward it.

Amy stopped in front of the pretty little upright piano, smiling as she saw where a cloth had been whisked over the shiny dark wood, leaving an edging of dust.

Hesitating a moment, she reached out tentatively and raised the lid covering the keys. Unable to resist, she held the lid in one hand and tinkled the ivory keys with the fingertips of the other.

"Do you play?"

"Oh!" Amy gasped, dropping the lid. Her fingertips barely escaped being struck. She spun around to see Blue walking slowly toward her. "You startled me," she said, splaying one hand on her racing heart.

Blue stopped in front of her. "Sorry." He nodded once at the piano. "Do you play?"

"A bit," she said, smiling. "Not enough to get excited about. I assume you play, since the piano is here."

"Nope. I bought it at an estate sale about six

months ago. The ranch next to mine called the Bar
None was sold for back taxes, and the furnishings,
equipment, everything on the place, had to go.

"The piano was a steal, but when you get right
down to it, I don't have a single reason to own it. It
just sits there gathering dust like everything else."
He shrugged. "Oh, well."

"I saw a Sold sign in front of that ranch."

Blue nodded. "I know, but it's still sitting empty.
It's too bad, because there's good land over there
going to waste. Did you get settled in?"

"Yes. The bedroom and bath are lovely. Thank
you." Amy paused. "Do you have time to answer a
few questions?"

"Not really. Do you ride?" Blue asked. *Say no,
Amy. The correct answer is some form of no.*

Amy frowned. "Ride what?"

Bingo. "Oh, boy," he said, chuckling. "If you
have to ask, then you don't."

"Pardon me?"

"Have you ever ridden a horse, Amy?"

"No, not really, but how tough can it be?"

Blue started to retort, then smiled and shook his
head instead.

Perfect, he thought. This was going exactly the
way he'd hoped it would.

"Right," he finally said. "How tough can it be?
You just plant your bottom on the saddle and ride
off into the sunset."

"Makes sense to me," Amy said pleasantly.

"Fine. So let's go for a short ride, shall we? I can show you some of the ranch."

"Splendid," Amy said, beaming. "I'll just dash back to my room and get my recorder. It clips to my belt loop so I'll have both hands free when I need them."

"That's just dandy."

A few minutes later, Amy had the small recorder attached snugly to a belt loop on her jeans. She followed Blue down a hallway that led to the kitchen.

"Ignore the mess," Blue said. "I managed to dust and vacuum a little before you came, but I still need to do some scrubbin' and rubbin' here in the kitchen."

Amy glanced around quickly. The kitchen was a large, sunny room, decorated in yellow and pale orange. The appliances were modern, and there was an oval oak table surrounded by eight captain's chairs.

The sinks and countertops were filled with dirty dishes.

"It's not as bad as it looks," Blue said, slowing his step. "A couple of go-throughs with the dishwasher will solve the whole problem." He laughed. "Besides, I'm running out of clean dishes."

Blue's deep, throaty laughter was so richly male, it was sinful, Amy thought. The man's charm just didn't quit.

"Wouldn't it be efficient to hire a housekeeper?" Amy said as they entered a room beyond the kitchen.

"Probably," Blue said. "This is the mud room."

"Wait, wait," Amy said. She snatched the recorder from her belt loop, pressed the On button and held the device toward Blue. "Okay, this is the mud room. And?"

"And nothing," he said, frowning. "This is the mud room. End of bulletin."

"What does one do in a mud room?"

"Wash off mud and...stuff."

"Oh." Amy brought the recorder close to her lips. "Mud room is beyond the kitchen and leads to the outside. It has a utility sink, shelving unit with towels and cleaning supplies, hat rack and a pegboard holding rain slickers and jackets of varying weights." She looked at Blue. "What's that gizmo on the floor by the door?"

"A boot jack to help remove boots."

"Got it." She snapped off the recorder and reattached it to her jeans. "All set."

"Whatever," Blue said with a shrug. "I'm sure the populace of Houston will be thrilled down to their socks to have been given the inside scoop on what a mud room looks like."

Amy glared at Blue, then followed him out the back door.

The sky was a pale blue with thin stripes of white clouds. A cool breeze was blowing in erratic puffs, as though trying to decide whether to make the effort to become a whipping wind or to fizzle out and be done with it.

Blue strolled leisurely toward the barn, and Amy

fell in step beside him. She inhaled deeply, cataloging the aroma of sweet hay and what she assumed was the pungent scent of horses and cattle.

She produced the recorder again and asked Blue to state how many acres of land made up the Rocking B and the number of cattle grazing there. He answered her questions in a monotone, definitely sounding bored.

"Can't you write this stuff down?" Blue said as she clipped the recorder back into place. "That recorder is going to get on my nerves very quickly."

"It's the most efficient means by which to gather my data. I'll type the information into my computer tonight. At the end of the week, I'll run a hard copy of the notes, and from that printout I'll write the story A Week In The Life Of A Texas Rancher."

"Wow," Blue said dryly. "I bet people will be late to work on the day it hits the stands. The column will be so fascinating, they won't be able to put it down."

"You certainly have a negative attitude," Amy said. "Don't you enjoy being a rancher, Blue?"

He halted dead in his tracks and turned to face her, splaying one large hand on his chest.

"*I* do, yes, of course, or I wouldn't be here. Believe me, no one would make this their life work if they didn't like it. Glamorous and exciting, it is not.

"The thing is, Amy, a suit-and-tie type in the city won't give a rip about what takes place day to day on a ranch. I don't care what Gib McKinley originally said, I'm sure he'd listen to reason and allow you to scratch this and pick a different occupation for your story.''

She would be delighted to do so, Amy thought. She certainly wasn't enthused about Gib McKinley's dumb brainstorm. Blue realized the whole interview had been Gib's idea, but he seemed to think she still had a voice in the matter. What he wasn't totally aware of was that she had absolutely no choice but to stay put and do as she'd been told. She had no intention, however, of letting Blue Bishop in on that extremely depressing fact.

''Of course Gib would take my opinion into consideration, but you're wrong, Blue,'' she said brightly. ''People will find all of this very interesting.''

''Right,'' he muttered, then started off again.

Near the barn, Blue stopped walking.

''I'll give you a thorough tour of the barn later,'' he said. ''Wait here a minute, and I'll get the horses I saddled so we can go for a ride.''

Amy nodded absently as she swept her gaze over the corrals and adjacent buildings. She made a mental note to ask Blue what each structure was used for.

A short time later, the snort of a horse caused her to snap her head around, and her eyes widened at what she saw.

Blue was leading two horses by the reins.

One was sleek and black, with a white streak down its nose.

But what on earth was that other thing? Amy wondered. It was huge—tall and fat, with bulging sides. It was plodding along, as though each step might be its last, and its eyes were half-closed, giving the impression it had either just awakened from a nap or was about to go to sleep. It was the biggest, ugliest so-called horse she'd ever seen.

"This is Snazzy," Blue said, nodding toward the horse in question. "She's perfect for someone without a great deal of riding experience."

"But—"

"She's a bit...wide, but you shouldn't be too uncomfortable. Snazzy is the safest horse for you, Amy. Ready to ride?"

Not on your life, Bishop, Amy mentally yelled.

"Certainly, Blue," she said, smiling sweetly. "Whatever you say."

Chapter Three

An hour later, Blue glanced over for the umpteenth time at Amy, who was perched in the saddle on Snazzy.

Chaps had emerged from the barn with a Stetson for Amy to wear, and the too-big hat rested just above her eyebrows, causing her to look like a terrified little girl. As they plodded slowly along, she was clutching the reins and saddle horn with both hands, in a death grip.

Hell, Blue thought, he couldn't handle any more of this. If Amy had whined, hollered or complained in some manner, he would figure riding Snazzy was Amy's just deserts for insisting on staying at the Rocking B.

But she hadn't said one word since he'd helped her up onto the ridiculous horse. Not a peep, not a moan, not a whimper...nothing.

He felt horrible for making her ride on the fattest, most uncomfortable horse that he owned.

He was a jerk, and in contrast Amy was a tough, feisty lady who at the moment had earned his utmost respect.

"There's a watering hole in those cottonwood trees up ahead," Blue said. "Let's rest a bit."

Amy nodded, no readable expression on her face.

Rest? she mentally echoed. Resting wouldn't do any good. She would have to die to end her agony. She ached from the tips of her toes to the top of her curly hair. There was not one hidden, or forgotten, place in her body that wasn't screaming for mercy.

But she wasn't going to die. Oh, no, not yet, because she had people to murder first. She would strangle Gibson McKinley, then Blue Bishop, then Snazzy the horse and finally Sue Ann for being on *their* side by declaring that cowboys in tight jeans and sexy Stetsons were wonderful.

"Whoa, there," Blue said, interrupting Amy's mental list of those to be eliminated.

Blue reached over and tugged gently on Snazzy's reins, bringing the huge animal to a halt. Swinging out of the saddle, he allowed the reins to trail on the ground, then came around to stand next to Amy.

"I'll help you down," he said. "Just drop the

reins. Snazzy won't go anywhere. Swing your leg over, and I'll grip you by the waist.''

Amy let go of the reins as instructed, but she didn't budge.

''Hello?'' Blue said.

Amy peered at him from beneath the brim of the huge Stetson, her eyes as wide as saucers.

''I can't move,'' she said. ''I think I *did* die, but the message hasn't reached my brain yet.''

''I'm definitely a jerk,'' Blue mumbled.

''Pardon me?''

''Nothing.''

In the next instant, Blue reached up, planted his hands on Amy's waist and lifted her from the saddle.

''Wait,'' Amy yelled as she whizzed through the air, her Stetson flying in the opposite direction.

Blue planted her feet on the ground and released her. The moment he let go, Amy began to crumple. Blue's arms shot out, and he lifted her into his arms, holding her tightly to his chest.

Amy turned her head to look at Blue and found herself staring into his incredible sapphire blue eyes, which were now only inches away.

''You've cut off the circulation to your legs,'' Blue said. ''You'll be fine in a few minutes.''

Legs? Amy thought, still gazing into Blue's eyes. What legs? Whose legs? Oh! *Her* legs.

''I see,'' she said. ''Well, it's certainly nice to know that I'll walk again. Why don't you put me down in the grass by that tree there, and I'll sit and anticipate the return of my legs to my body.''

Body, Blue thought with keen awareness. He was attempting, and failing miserably, to ignore how sensational Amy's slender, soft, womanly body felt in his arms, nestled close to his chest. She smelled good, like sunshine, soap and flowers.

''Put you down,'' Blue repeated, his voice slightly gritty. ''Good idea.''

As Blue carried her toward the grass, Amy savored the moment. This was how Scarlett must have felt, she decided, when Rhett swept her into his arms and charged up the huge staircase at Tara.

She was acutely aware of her own femininity in comparison to Blue's rugged masculinity.

For a tick of time, she did nothing but simply *be.* She was cradled in the powerful arms of a man who was capable of standing between her and harm's way, who could protect her and keep the stress and pressures of the world at bay.

It was heavenly.

She was going to remember this moment. It was hers to keep. In her reality, she was independent, focused on her career, had her future mapped out in precise detail. There was no room for a man, a husband, home, children. No room. She knew that, and accepted it.

But for a second, she'd been Scarlett O'Hara in the arms of Rhett Butler, and she would tuck the memory away carefully in a treasure chest in her heart and mind.

Blue set Amy down gently in the thick, fragrant grass. As the horses wandered to the edge of the watering hole for a drink, he sank to the ground next to her, resting his back against a tree.

Amy sat with her legs extended, wiggling her tennis-shoe-clad toes.

"They're coming alive," she said.

"Amy," Blue said quietly, "I'm sorry."

She looked up at him quickly, frowning in confusion. "For what? It's not your fault that I've never ridden a horse before."

"But it *is* my fault that you were riding one that was much too big for you. I have a smaller mare that would have been far more comfortable. I deliberately made things difficult for you because I was ticked off at myself for agreeing to allow you to come here. I apologize for my behavior."

A strange warmth fluttered around Amy's heart as she stared at Blue.

She had never before met a man like Blue Bishop. The majority of men she was acquainted with were caught up in machismo posturing, strutting their stuff, continually trying to impress each other and the women around them.

But Blue? He was apologizing, for heaven's sake, for conducting himself in a less than gentlemanly manner, admitting that he'd taken out his frustration on her.

Blue did not appear the least bit concerned that he was rendering himself totally vulnerable to whatever reaction she might have to his confession and apology. He was stripped bare, had dropped the macho cloak he protected himself with.

Blue Bishop was a confusing, intriguing and compelling man. He was throwing her completely off kilter by behaving so differently from what she was accustomed to.

Oh, dear, Amy thought, on top of being so unsettled by not having enough time to properly prepare for this assignment, she was now dealing with a man who was not behaving true to form.

She didn't know whether to hug him or hit him!

She should be so angry at Blue for the stunt he'd pulled, his attempt to get her to hightail it back to town, but it was impossible to be mad at a man who was being so open and honest about his wrongdoing.

"Amy?" Blue said. "Do you accept my apology?"

"What? Oh, yes, of course, and I thank you for making it. You're an...an unusual man, Blue."

He chuckled. "Unusual? I've been called worse, I suppose."

"That was a compliment," Amy said softly.

Blue's smile faded. "Yeah, I know it was. I don't deserve it, but thank you. You're not bad yourself. You rode Snazzy without one word of complaint. You're a class act, Amy Madison."

Big brown eyes were looking directly into sapphire blue ones, and time stopped. There were no trees, or grass, or horses. There was nothing beyond the sudden, sensual awareness crackling between them, creating leaping flames of instantaneous desire within them.

Amy tore her gaze from Blue's, picked a blade of grass with trembling fingers, then focused her full attention on it.

"It's my understanding," she said, hoping her voice was steadier than it sounded to her, "that ranchers often speak in terms of sections in regard to land, sections being mathematically convertible into acres, or miles."

Amy fiddled with the blade of grass, not looking at Blue as she waited for him to comment on her statement.

Silent seconds ticked by. Amy slid a tentative glance at Blue from beneath her lashes, only to discover he was looking directly at her. Flustered, she dropped the blade of grass, then lifted her chin and met Blue's gaze.

"Right, Mr. Bishop?" she asked. "It is sections, isn't it? I'm certain my data is correct, but I'd appreciate your verifying the information I've just presented."

Blue nodded slowly, then shoved his Stetson up with one thumb, his eyes never leaving hers.

"The information you presented, Ms. Madison," he said, his voice deep and rumbly, "is that you want to kiss me as much as I want to kiss you. That came across loud and clear.''

Amy's mouth dropped open in shock at the same instant her eyes widened. She drew in a gulp of air, then narrowed her gaze.

''That's absurd,'' she retorted none too quietly. ''Blue Bishop, you have got to be one of the most conceited men I've ever had the displeasure of meeting. Do you always assume that every woman who crosses your path is eager to kiss the living daylights out of you?''

Blue grinned. ''Nope.''

''I should hope not,'' she said with an indignant little sniff.

''Some want my entire body.''

''That does it,'' she said, scrambling to her feet. ''You're not only conceited, you're despicable.'' She paused. ''Oh! Ow! Oh!'' She hopped on one foot, then the other. ''My toes, my feet, my legs... Ow! They feel like there's pins sticking in them.''

Blue leaned forward, grasped one of Amy's hands and tugged.

''Hey, sit down,'' he said. ''You have to wait until the circulation has returned completely to your legs and feet. Amy, sit.''

Blue had caught Amy's hand in midhop, and the tug caused her to lose her balance. As she toppled over, Blue dropped her hand and caught her, planting her sideways across his thighs.

"Just relax for a few more minutes," he said, "and you'll be fine. Stay put and relax."

Relax! Amy thought. Blue was certifiably insane if he thought she could sit in his lap, on those strong, muscled thighs of his, and carry on a casual conversation about anything.

This entire situation was out of control. *She* was out of control, and things were definitely going from bad to worse.

The infuriating truth was that Blue had been right about her wanting to kiss him. During that strange, tension-laden interlude, when she'd been pinned in place by those damnable blue eyes of his, she'd had a fleeting image of pressing her lips to Blue's.

And the mortifying thing was, he knew it!

She suddenly realized that she was erasing every nice thought she'd had regarding Blue Bishop's willingness to apologize for sticking her on top of that fat horse.

In actuality, Blue was as conceited as the day was long. He was a hunk who was accustomed to women falling all over him, and his macho ego was bigger than the state of Texas.

Well, he wasn't dealing with a bubble brain here. No, sir, Amy Madison was in charge of Amy Madison, and she could dish out as good as she got. In her estimation, Mr. Bishop needed to be taken down a peg or two.

"I guess you're right," she said pleasantly. "My legs weren't quite ready to support me yet. I'll just sit here and relax, just like you said. But I do need to get a teeny, tiny bit more comfortable.''

Amy wiggled one way, paused, then wiggled again, finally nodding in satisfaction. She folded her hands primly in her lap, stared into space, then wiggled her bottom one more time for good measure.

Blue was on fire. A coil of heat was tightening low in his aroused body, hot, burning, from the maneuvers of Amy's delectable bottom.

She *knew* what she was doing to him with her wiggling, the little minx. She was paying him back in spades for his cocky remark about women always wanting his body. Ms. Madison was giving him tit for tat. He liked her spunk—he really did.

Amy shifted on his lap again.

''Enough,'' he said, moaning and laughing at the same time. ''I was kidding about women standing in line to get at my body. Joking, you know? Lord, woman, sit still.''

Amy batted her eyelashes. ''But, sir, I'm only attempting to get comfy. Do you have a problem of some sort?''

''Ma'am,'' Blue said, chuckling, ''due to where you are presently perched, you are very aware of exactly what my problem is.''

Amy's cheeks warmed. She knew she was blushing, and only hoped that Blue wouldn't notice.

''You're blushing,'' he said with a hoot of laughter. ''I didn't know women still did that. I love it.''

He paused, still smiling. "Well, here we are. What's next?"

"Nothing," Amy said, starting to move off his lap.

Blue circled her waist with one arm, holding her firmly in place.

"Wait a minute," he said seriously. "Amy, I really was joking about all the women wanting my body. You were being so all business, with your cute nose poked in the air, and I couldn't resist giving you a bad time. You paid me back...royally."

"Well, I—" Amy started.

"However," Blue interrupted, "I meant it when I said you wanted to kiss me as much as I wanted to kiss you. That part was *not* a joke, not even close. Am I right?"

"I prefer not to discuss this," she said, refusing to meet his gaze.

"Why not? We're two perfectly normal people who felt a desire to kiss each other. There's nothing wrong with that."

Amy looked at him. "There certainly is something wrong with that. I'm here as a journalist on assignment. And you were absolutely correct in stating that I'm all business, Mr. Bishop, and I'd appreciate your remembering that during my stay here on your ranch. If you should forget, I'll be only too happy to remind you."

She slid off of Blue's lap and got to her feet.

"I see," he said slowly. "That's very interesting." He rolled to his feet, then tugged his Stetson low.

"Yep, very, very interesting." He whistled, causing the horses to raise their heads. "The thing is…" He whistled again, and both horses started toward him.

"What?" Amy said, frowning. "The thing is…?"

Blue produced a very male, very sexy smile.

"The thing is," he said, "who is going to remind *you*, Ms. Madison?"

Amy searched her brain frantically for a snappy retort, a dynamite comeback that would put Blue Bishop firmly in his place, but her mind was a total blank.

She spun around, snatched up her hat from the ground and started off, glancing at Blue over one shoulder.

"I'll walk back to the house, thank you," she said, hoping she sounded borderline haughty.

"That was my plan exactly," Blue said, nodding. "I figured we'd both walk, and I'd lead the horses." He paused. "There's just one thing, Amy," he added, raising his voice as she trekked farther away.

"What's that?" she yelled, not stopping.

"You're going in the wrong direction."

Oh…drat, Amy thought, coming to a halt. Just when she was certain this situation couldn't get any worse…it did.

Her shoulders slumped, and fatigue consumed her from head to toe. She turned and stomped back to where Blue stood holding the horses' reins.

"Lead on, Bishop," Amy said, sweeping one arm in the air. "I'll make a note of the fact that a person can become easily lost on ranch land, due to the fact that it's all dull, drab terrain, and looks the same as far as the eye can see.''

"Hey, that's not true. Texas ranch land is beautiful. It's clean, uncluttered, some of nature's finest work. I'm going to be really ticked off if you say rotten things about the Rocking B in your column.''

"You tend to your ranch," Amy said ever so sweetly, "and I'll tend to my column. Shall we go?''

As they walked, Blue mentally shook his head in disbelief.

Amy Madison had gotten the last word, he realized incredulously. How had that happened? He was accustomed to having the edge in any given situation. He was definitely going to have to stay on his toes during the duration of feisty Ms. Madison's visit.

Amy was a handful, he mused, unable to curb an appreciative smile. He had a feeling a man would never be bored if he was involved in a relationship with her.

Relationship?

Blue slid a glance at Amy as she walked beside him, managing not to chuckle aloud at the very cute picture she presented with the huge Stetson resting nearly on her ears.

Bishop, you're slipping, man, he told himself. He'd been so hot under the collar about being roped into having a nuisance of a reporter on his spread, he'd failed to consider his ongoing mission.

He wanted, was seriously searching for, intended to have...a wife.

Amy was an attractive, intelligent, unattached young woman. He should, therefore, be automatically viewing her as a possible candidate for being Mrs. Blue Bishop.

Many months ago, he and his brothers, Bram and Tux, had decided it was time to exit the swinging-singles' scene. They'd agreed they were overdue for hearth and home, wife and babies.

What they *hadn't* known was how damn difficult it was to find a suitable wife among the endless stream of women who were in, then out, of their lives. The whole endeavor had turned out to be frustrating as hell.

His older brother, Tux, had finally accomplished the goal and was happily married to his Incredibly Beautiful Nancy—as the brothers called her—the lucky son of a gun.

But as for his twin brother, Bram, and himself, hell, they were batting zero in the finding-a-wife program.

Blue narrowed his eyes in concentration.

He had to regroup, rethink his reaction to Amy being at the Rocking B. For now, he would forget about shipping her out in twenty-four, or forty-eight, hours. She was scheduled to stay a week, and that was good. The more time he had to discover all he could about Amy, from the major to the mundane, the better.

Amy Madison would have enough information for ten columns on a week in the life of a Texas rancher, because he was going to keep her Super Glued to him every waking hour of the day.

And the nights?

Whoa, Bishop.

He had to take things slow and easy. Seduction in its purest form belonged to bygone days of playing the singles' game.

When viewing a woman as a possible partner for life, one had to mind one's manners, be gentlemanly, romantic, bring out the softness, the womanliness, in said candidate, if there was any of either to rise to the fore, Blue reminded himself. Lord, he was brilliant sometimes.

"So, Amy," Blue said pleasantly, "tell me about yourself. You know, where you grew up, why you chose to be a reporter, the whole bit."

"No."

Blue frowned. "No? Why not?"

"Because talking about me wouldn't be productive. The subject matter is *you* and what takes place on the Rocking B during an average week."

"But..."

Amy took the recorder from her belt loop, clicked it on, then shot her arm straight up in the air.

"Please speak loud and clear, Blue," she said. "Did you know as a child that you wanted to own a ranch? Or was it a decision you made, say, in college? Just chatter your little heart out. Inquiring minds want to know.''

"Well, hell,'' Blue said.

One thing was certain, he thought. *His* inquiring mind had a rough road to go in discovering what he wanted to know about Amy Madison.

Chapter Four

During the stroll back to the barn, Amy learned that Blue had decided when he was six years old that he was going to be a cowboy when he grew up. From that day on, he had never wavered from achieving that goal.

"Do you always get what you go after?" Amy asked.

Blue smiled slightly. "Usually. My brothers and I are very determined individuals, always have been. We set our sights on something, and it's generally a done deal within a reasonable length of time."

Except for finding a wife, he thought glumly. There was nothing reasonable at all about how difficult that was proving to be.

"How many men work on the Rocking B?" Amy asked.

"Five, including me. Chaps was here when I bought the spread about ten years ago. He can't handle long days in the saddle anymore, so he's in charge of the barn, the tack room, and keeps everything shipshape. He has his own place to live at the end of the barn. The other three guys are in the bunkhouse."

"Do you have a cook for them?"

"No, we're not big enough for that. They fix their own meals in the bunkhouse kitchen. I take care of myself." Blue paused. "Amy, I swear, this is boring as dirt. Your readers won't give a rip about who makes our breakfast."

"I'll be the judge of that," she said firmly. "Besides, I won't necessarily use everything we discuss. I always end up with more data than I need. Better to have too much than too little, you know?"

"Do you have any brothers and sisters?" Blue asked, sliding a glance at her.

"No. Let's talk about your use of windmills, shall we? Windmills, by the way, were first used in Europe in the twelfth century and..."

Amy's dissertation was interrupted by the approach of a horse and rider speeding in their direction.

"It's Tinker," Blue said, frowning.

"Tinker?"

"He's a genius with motors, anything that runs. He tinkers, get it?

"Hey, Tink," Blue yelled, "what's up?"

Tinker was in his late twenties, was tall and skinny and had carrot-colored hair. He pulled the horse to a halt about ten feet in front of Amy and Blue.

"Some fence is down on the north range, boss," Tinker said. "We've got a dozen head of cattle scattered from here to Toledo."

"Hell," Blue said. "Amy, I've got to go. Just hold Snazzy's reins, walk ahead of her and she'll follow. You can see the barn in the distance, so you won't get lost. Hand Snazzy over to Chaps. I'll catch up with you later at the house."

"But..."

Blue swung onto the saddle of his horse.

"Let's go, Tink," he said.

"But..." Amy said again, then coughed from the billow of dust created by the departing horses.

Amy sighed, picked up Snazzy's reins, then trudged on.

When she finally reached the barn, she was greeted by Chaps. He was friendly but, as Amy soon discovered, a man of few words. Her attempt at conversation was met by two nods, one "Yep," three "Nopes" and a "Mmm." Defeated, she wandered back into the house.

After she showered and put on clean clothes, Amy decided she might survive her ordeal on Snazzy after all. She entered the kitchen to hopefully find makings for a sandwich.

"Ugh," she muttered, glancing around the large room. "I forgot this was a disaster area."

After managing to construct a peanut-butter-and-jelly sandwich on the edge of the cluttered counter, she ate it standing up, then added a glass of milk to the meal.

She was not, she told herself, cleaning this kitchen. She was a journalist, not a maid. If Blue Bishop had a problem preparing his dinner in this chaos, so be it.

She made it all the way to the kitchen door before stopping and throwing up her hands.

Drat, she thought. Blue was out there rounding up roaming cattle, fixing a fence and doing heaven only knew what else. Her body was crying for a nap. Her mind said she should do more research with her hidden library books. Her conscience was poking her with nagging insistence that she should use part of her unasked-for idle hours to set the kitchen to rights.

She spun around and marched back to the dishwasher, opening it with more force than was necessary.

Several hours later, Amy planted her hands on her hips and scrutinized the kitchen. A smile touched her lips as she nodded in satisfaction.

The counters were clear, every dish, glass, cup and handfuls of silverware washed and put away. She'd wiped down the appliances, cabinet fronts and table, and had swept the floor.

She'd found a chicken and a bag of vegetables in the freezer, defrosted them in the microwave, then put them in a pan to slow-bake in the oven.

The table was set for two for a dinner that would include a dessert of pudding served in pretty glasses she'd found on a top shelf in one of the cupboards.

"Nice work," she said, "if I do say so myself."

Somewhere in the midst of her activities, she'd realized she was thoroughly enjoying herself. It had nothing to do with being a Henrietta Housewife type. No way. She didn't have a domestic bone in her body, despite the loving teachings of her mother during her childhood.

No, the pleasure of her accomplishments came from the fact that she'd put her organizational skills, her eye for detail, and her ability to start with virtually nothing and produce excellence into operation.

Everything she had done in Blue Bishop's kitchen was a result of her applying her expertise as a journalist to a challenging situation. Her success simply reinforced her dedication to her career.

Amy inhaled the delicious aroma of baking chicken, then headed for her bedroom to do some reading from the books in her secret stash under the bed.

An hour later, Blue entered the mud room, removed his boots, placed his Stetson on the hat rack, then entered the kitchen. He stopped in his tracks so suddenly, he teetered for a moment, his eyes widening at what he saw.

Walking tentatively forward, he swept his astonished gaze over the area. As he peered in the oven, his mouth watered at the sight and smell of the browning chicken and vegetables. His stomach rumbled, reminding him he hadn't eaten since a very early breakfast.

Amy had done all this, he thought. Incredible. He'd put in a hard day on the range, and had come home to dinner in the oven and a kitchen that was sparkling clean. Man, he'd died and gone to heaven.

He had to find Amy.

But first, he had to think about what he was going to say.

Amy had declared in no uncertain terms that she was going to be all business while at the Rocking B. She was a journalist, nothing more. In other words, there would be no kissin' under the cottonwood trees, or any other hanky-panky.

But, Blue realized, Amy had obviously had a change of mind. Why else would she have cleaned the grungy kitchen and fixed dinner? Her message was clear. She wanted him to view her as a woman, not just a reporter.

Fantastic!

Easy, Bishop, he told himself. He had to take this slow and easy. He had no idea if he should compliment Amy for twenty minutes, rave on and on about what he'd discovered in his kitchen or play it loose and cool, thank her once and let that be that.

What did Amy want him to do?

Blue dragged one hand through his tousled, sweat-drenched hair.

Women were so damn complicated. They hadn't been complicated when he was part of the singles' scene. Not at all. They had only become complicated when he decided he wanted to get married, wanted a wife and children.

Maybe he would postpone finding Amy for a bit so he could think about this some more, Blue thought. He definitely needed a shower and clean clothes.

With a decisive nod, Blue headed for his bedroom, smiling at Amy's closed bedroom door as he passed it.

Amy sat propped against the pillows on her bed, her computer on her lap, books opened around her on the spread. She glanced at a page, then her fingers flew over the computer keys.

A moment later, her hands stilled in midair and her head snapped up as she heard the sound of running water in the distance.

Blue was home.

She pressed the button on the computer to save the material she'd typed, closed the machine, then scrambled off the bed. Within minutes, the books were once more hidden in the tote bag beneath the bed. She combed her hair, freshened her lipstick and headed for the kitchen.

Blue finished dressing, then started toward the bedroom door. Hesitating, he spun around, went to the telephone on the nightstand next to the bed, snatched up the receiver and punched in some numbers.

"Be there," he muttered to himself.

"Yo!"

"Bram? Man, I'm glad I caught you."

"Just walked in the door. What's doin', Blue?"

Blue sank onto the edge of the bed, glanced at the bedroom door and lowered his voice.

"Just listen, okay?"

"Why are you whispering?" Bram whispered.

"Shut up and listen."

"Right."

"Due to the fact that I can't say no to our mother any better than you and Tux can, I have a reporter from the *Holler* here for a week, gathering information for a column on being a rancher."

"Ah, fame and glory comes to my twin brother," Bram said. "Can I have your autograph?"

"Damn it, Bram, this is serious."

"Sorry. Go ahead. But talk fast, would you? I'm a starving man."

"Yeah, me, too, but this comes before food. The reporter is a woman named Amy Madison. I was so ticked about getting roped into this thing that it took me a while to realize that Amy should definitely be viewed as a candidate for a wife.''

''Hey, we're supposed to be on red alert at all times for those candidates, Blue.''

''I know, I know, but I'd forgotten when she first arrived. Anyway, she's pretty, really cute, and smart, and feisty, and has a sense of humor, and— Well, you get the picture.''

''I'll take her. Send her right over, and I'll haul her off to city hall and marry her.''

''Bram!''

''Wrong answer, huh? So, you were saying…?''

''Amy made it clear that she is strictly business.''

''Bad attitude on the wife checklist, Blue.''

''But wait, there's more. She laid that on me, but when I got back to the house after rounding up some cattle, my kitchen—which was a dirty dish away from being condemned by the health department— was clean as a whistle and dinner was cooking in the oven.''

''No joke? Amy did all that?''

''Yep.''

''Whew. Heavy. She said she was nothing more than a reporter, then she does a really womanly number by cleaning the kitchen and cooking dinner.''

''Yeah. Bram, you've got to help me here. I hustled into my room to shower and change, so I haven't seen Amy yet. I don't know how to react to what she did. She's obviously trying to tell me that she

changed her mind about being viewed only as a journalist, but—''

"I see your problem. This calls for finesse, Blue.
But guess what? You and I aren't setting the world
on fire with our expertise in dealing with possible
wife candidates. Maybe we should call Tux. No, forget it. He'd laugh himself silly.''

"Bram, look, I've got two choices. I make a major
deal out of what Amy did, or I don't. Pick one.''

"Me? If you recall, there's no wedding band on
my left hand, brother.'' Bram paused. "Okay, here
goes. I've seen your kitchen. What Amy did was a
tremendous undertaking. Therefore, my instincts say
you should react to it big time in return. Make
sense?''

"How big of a big time?''

"Blue, how should I know? Just do what feels
natural and right. Hell, I'm exhausted. This finding-
a-wife stuff is hard work. I'm off this phone and into
some food. Good luck, keep me posted, it was
crummy talking to you, goodbye.''

"Bram, wait,'' Blue said, then swore under his
breath as he heard the dial tone buzzing in his ear.

He slammed the receiver into place, stood, took a
deep breath, let it out slowly, then squared his shoulders and left the bedroom.

Amy placed a platter containing the chicken and
vegetables on the table, then straightened and pressed
one hand over her thudding heart.

She was nervous, for Pete's sake, she fumed. She'd poked that poor chicken with a fork so many times to see if it was perfectly done, it could pass for a pin cushion. Then she'd arranged the vegetables around the dumb bird in alternating order, as though she was attempting to create a work of art.

Anyone watching her ridiculous performance would be convinced they were seeing a new bride preparing her first dinner for her groom.

Now *that* was really absurd. The last thing on earth she wanted was a husband. A home. Children. No, she'd made her life's choice…her career.

She had no intention of being pulled from the path toward her dream of becoming a top-notch, highly respected journalist.

She could *not* have a marriage and family, and still achieve her goal. To try to have both meant she would be mediocre in all the too-many roles she was attempting to function in.

Darn it, she *knew* all this. So why was she flustered over a stupid baked chicken, hoping Blue Bishop would enjoy the dinner she'd prepared?

She had no idea why she was behaving this way.

Of course, she realized suddenly with a sigh of relief. Her nutty behavior was due to the fact that she was exhausted. Yes, that had to be it. Lack of sleep was depriving her weary brain of the oxygen, or whatever, that would normally provide her with the means to perform in a familiar and rational manner.

Thank heavens she'd figured it out. She certainly felt better now.

"Hello, Amy."

Amy jumped, then turned to see Blue standing in the kitchen doorway. He was wearing jeans, white sport socks and a blue Western shirt that was the exact shade of his incredible blue eyes. His thick dark hair was damp from his shower, and his tanned skin looked like polished bronze. Gorgeous.

But what was Blue thinking? Amy wondered frantically. There was no readable expression on his face, no clue as to his reaction to her invading his kitchen.

Was he angry? Did he view her cleaning and cooking as being pushy and rude? Was "Hello, Amy" all he was going to say about what she had done?

"Hello, Blue," she said, hoping her voice hadn't been as squeaky as it sounded to her own ears.

Blue started toward her. Slowly. Very slowly.

Amy's heart quickened, and she took a step backward, feeling as though a sleek panther were advancing.

"I, um," she said, looking directly into Blue's eyes as he continued toward her. "I hope you don't mind that I... What I mean is..." She took a wobbly breath. "Blue?"

Do what feels natural and right, Blue's mind echoed.

He stopped in front of Amy, framed her face in his large hands, lowered his head and kissed her.

Amy's eyes widened in shock, and her hands flew

up to splay flat on Blue's rock-hard chest with every intention of pushing him away.

But Blue's lips...this kiss...the heat...oh, dear heaven, she was on fire. The kiss was like none before and was consuming her with desire. She couldn't think; she could only feel, and it was *ecstasy*.

Amy slid her hands upward to encircle Blue's neck, inching her fingertips into his damp hair, returning the ardor of his kiss in total abandon as her lashes drifted shut.

Blue dropped his hands from Amy's face and wrapped his arms around her, nestling her to him. Passion exploded within him as he felt her surrender to the kiss. He parted her lips and thrust his tongue into her mouth to meet her tongue.

Low in his body, tension coiled hotter, then hotter yet, his arousal heavy and full. He deepened the kiss even more, drinking of Amy's sweet taste, burning with the want of her, going up in flames.

Amy's breasts were crushed against Blue's chest, creating an exquisite near-pain that brought fleeting images of his soothing hands and lips on the throbbing flesh. Her tongue dueled seductively with his, dancing, stroking, fanning the fire within her into licking flames.

A niggling voice in her mind whispered disapproval of her actions, told her insistently that she was behaving out of character.

But Amy ignored the voice, pushed it away and

simply savored the sensations swirling throughout her, savored the feel, the taste, the aroma, of Blue. She inhaled his scent of soap and fresh air and man.

Moving her hands from his hair to his shoulders, she hazily relished the taut muscles beneath the crisp material of his shirt.

She was wonderously aware of every inch of her body, of her own femininity compared to Blue's magnificent masculinity. She felt so vibrantly alive, so womanly.

This kiss should, could, would, go on forever.

Amy Madison, the voice in her mind now yelled, *what in heaven's name are you doing?*

Amy's eyes flew open in horror, and she stiffened. She twisted away from Blue's embrace, unsteady on her feet. She drew a trembling breath, then wrapped her hands around her elbows in a protective gesture.

Blue shook his head slightly to clear the sensual mist consuming him. His breathing was rough, and he stared up at the ceiling for a moment, struggling for control of his heated, aroused body.

"Amy," he said finally, looking at her. He cleared his throat, took a deep breath and let it out slowly. "Amy, I—"

"No," she said, shaking her head. "Don't say anything. Not a word. Please. What just happened, didn't happen. Well, it happened, but it shouldn't have happened. Therefore, I'm totally erasing what happened from my memory bank."

She pressed her hands to her flushed cheeks.

"I'm babbling like an idiot," she said dismally.

"Amy—"

She flung out her arms. "Damn you, Blue Bishop. Why did you do that? How dare you just march in here and kiss me without so much as a by-your-leave? Just who in heaven's name do you think you are?"

"I'm Blue Bishop, ma'am," he said, a slow smile creeping onto his lips, "who just shared a dynamite kiss with a lovely lady."

He nodded. "Yep, that kiss was sensational." The smile grew into a heart-stopping grin. "As for *why* I kissed you? Well, you see, I was overwhelmed by what you did here."

He glanced quickly around the kitchen, then met Amy's troubled gaze again.

"I was at a loss for words," he went on. "So I expressed my gratitude, my heartfelt appreciation, in a manner that felt natural and right to me."

Amy narrowed her eyes. "I certainly would have hated to witness what would have taken place if I'd washed the windows."

Blue burst into laughter. "Interesting thought."

Oh, Amy Madison was dynamite, all right, in a delicate, pint-size, *very* womanly package, he thought. This lady was most definitely a viable candidate for a wife.

As of this moment, he was going to start gathering his data, finding out her values, beliefs, what made her tick, who Amy really was.

He might very well end up disappointed again, just as he had over the past months, but there was only one way to find out.

So far, he knew that he and Amy sent each other up in flames with a kiss. Oh, man, he would like to haul her into his arms and kiss her again. And again.

Hell, he wanted to make love with Amy Madison. Right now. He would lift her into his arms, carry her to his bed, see her reach for him, desire radiating from her big dark eyes.

He would be gentle, so careful, because she was tiny, would need to be treated like the finest crystal ever made. They would make sweet, slow love for hours, closing out the world, focusing only on each other.

He wanted to just open his mouth and tell Amy how very much he desired her, tell her what their kiss had done to him, but he couldn't.

"Chicken," Amy said.

"What?" Blue said, having been pulled abruptly from his sensuous thoughts. "I'm what!"

"Not you," she said crossly. She pointed to the table. "The chicken is getting cold. Do you want to eat dinner or not?"

"Oh, yeah, sure. It looks great. I'll pour some drinks. Want some milk?"

Amy sank onto one of the chairs at the table. "Whatever," she said. "Milk is fine." She sighed. "I'm so mortified, I could die. I just cannot believe what happened."

Blue frowned as he poured two glasses of milk, then carried them to the table. He placed one in front of each of their plates, then sat down opposite Amy. She was scowling at her spoon.

"Amy," Blue said quietly, "why are you being so hard on yourself? We shared a kiss. There's nothing wrong with that."

"It was wrong for *me*," she said, splaying one hand on her chest as she met his gaze. "I'm here at the Rocking B in a professional capacity, as a journalist researching a story."

Blue chuckled as he picked up the carving set and began to attack the chicken.

Research? his mind echoed. Oh, if Amy only knew what he was now determined to discover about her. He was going to find out, come hell or high water, if Amy Madison was meant to be Mrs. Blue Bishop.

"Well, Ms. Madison," he said, still smiling, "I'd say that the research conducted here in this kitchen as to whether or not you and I are attracted to each other was very thorough.

"We now know that we are, indeed, attracted to one another *and* that the result of a kiss shared between us sets off sparks that make the Fourth of July seem like dim doings. Want a drumstick from this bird?"

"I don't care. Just plunk something on my plate."

Blue transferred a serving of chicken to Amy's plate. She spooned a few vegetables next to it, then began to poke at the food with her fork.

"That's not much to eat," Blue said. "Have some more chicken."

"No, thank you, this is plenty," Amy said. "I'm not very hungry."

"Are you certain you don't want more?"

"Positive."

Blue nodded, set his plate to one side, then pulled the platter in front of him.

"No sense in using a plate that doesn't need using," he said. "I'll just polish off the rest of this."

"Gracious," Amy said with a bubble of laughter. "I guess you're still a growing boy."

Blue captured one of Amy's hands with one of his own on the top of the table. She looked at him questioningly, seeing the serious expression on his face.

"No, Amy," he said, "I'm not a boy, I'm a man. And you're a woman. We *shared* a kiss that was sensational, and where it might lead remains to be seen. Nothing is wrong here. Nothing."

"But—"

"Enough said on the subject for now. Okay? And, Amy? Thank you very much for preparing this meal and cleaning the kitchen."

"You're very welcome, Blue," she said softly, pulling her hand slowly from beneath his. "I made pudding for dessert."

"Perfect," he said, looking directly into her eyes. "Absolutely perfect."

Chapter Five

Amy smacked her pillow, then flopped over onto her back on the bed, staring up at a ceiling she couldn't see in the midnight darkness.

She couldn't sleep! She was exhausted to the bone, absolutely dead tired, but thoughts kept chasing through her mind, one after the next, tumbling into a confusing, frustrating maze. She was so angry with herself, she could scream.

Blue Bishop, Amy fumed. He was the most exasperating man she'd ever met. He was so darn unpredictable. One minute he was cocky and borderline arrogant, then the next second there was true sincerity radiating from those damnable blue eyes of his.

Oh, merciful saints, those eyes.

And, of course, The Kiss, which had now taken on capital-letter importance.

The remembrance of The Kiss with Blue was driving her crazy. It had been an unbelievable kiss. *Divine.*

She would never, Amy knew, forget that kiss or the sensual sensations that had swirled throughout her, the feel, the taste, the aroma, of Blue. Never.

But, dear heaven, it had been so *wrong,* so out of character, so unprofessional. She had an entire week to spend at the Rocking B with Blue, and there would be no repeat performance of what had happened in the kitchen.

Have you got that, Amy Madison? she scolded herself.

What had Blue said? Oh, yes, that The Kiss had been sensational, and it remained to be seen where it might lead.

Ha! No way. Where it was leading was nowhere, because as far as she was concerned, she *was* going to erase it from her memory.

With a moan, Amy rolled onto her stomach. The Kiss *had* been a major happening, an unsettling experience, because of the powerfully sensuous impact it had had on her.

She hadn't wished for the kiss to end.

And she'd wanted more. She'd wanted to make love with Blue Bishop.

There, she'd admitted it, put it right out on the

table in her mind where she had no choice but to face the fact head-on and deal with it.

Well, fine. She had her data. Blue Bishop was a very dangerous man, a threat to her peace of mind, her long-established plans and goals for her life, her career. By knowing that, she was once more in control of herself.

She was now capable of completing her assignment for the *Holler* without succumbing to Blue's masculine magnetism, because she would stay on her toes, erect a barrier between herself and Blue that would protect her from him...and from her own feminine responses to him.

Amy Madison was back in charge of the fate and future of Amy Madison.

And now, she thought foggily, she could sleep.

It seemed to Amy that she had no sooner drifted off into blissful slumber than she was jerked awake by a steady knocking on the bedroom door.

"What!" she yelled, not opening her eyes.

"Rise and shine," Blue sang out through the closed door. "Breakfast is on the table in ten minutes. I let you sleep in. It's already five-thirty."

"Forget it," Amy mumbled. "Go ride a horse or milk a cow, Blue Bishop."

"Amy?"

"Yes!" she hollered. "I'm up."

"Ten minutes."

Muttering under her breath in disjointed sentences

regarding the minuscule amount of sleep she'd had, the rudeness of cowboys who beat on a person's door in the middle of the night and the fact that she hated breakfast, Amy shuffled into the bathroom.

Hoping a shower would revive her, Amy realized as she dressed in jeans and a long-sleeved green T-shirt that it hadn't worked. She was tired. She was cranky. She wanted to go home to her own little apartment and sleep for a week.

When she entered the kitchen, she was greeted by the aroma of brewing coffee and frying bacon. The first light of dawn was beginning to peek through the windows. She slumped onto a chair, folded her arms on the top of the table and cradled her head on the T-shirt-covered pillow.

Blue glanced over at her from where he was frying bacon at the stove, and chuckled.

"You don't look like a rise-and-shine person, Ms. Madison," he said. "Are you awake?"

"Mmm."

"Look at the bright side. I'm up at 4:00 a.m. in the summer. I push it up to five during the winter. How do you like your eggs?"

"Left in the refrigerator," came the muffled reply. "I have coffee and coffee for breakfast."

"Now, now, Amy, where's your journalistic authenticity this morning? You're doing a column on the week in the life of a Texas rancher, remember? You have to get with the program. A rancher always has a big, hearty breakfast to start his day."

"Yuck."

Blue chuckled again as he forked the bacon onto a pad of paper towels.

It really didn't matter if Amy ate a big morning meal, he thought. She wasn't going to be burning up the energy that he and his men would today. He would serve Ms. Madison a breakfast of coffee and coffee, per her half asleep half awake request.

He'd been waiting for Amy's appearance in the kitchen with a sense of anticipation bordering on the adolescent. He'd also spent a tossing-and-turning night, due to the desire for Amy still causing tight coils of heat to torment him low and hot in his body.

Oh, yeah, Amy Madison was getting to him, all right. Physically, he was a tied-in-knots wreck. Mentally? Well, he liked Amy—he really did. Every adjective he'd clicked off on a list about her for Bram had been true.

But there was so much more that he wanted—needed—to know. How did Amy feel about marriage? Children? What impression was she getting so far about life on a ranch?

The final part probably wasn't scoring too well. All she'd really experienced was a mess of a kitchen and a ride on the fattest horse in the county.

The problem was, there really wasn't a glamorous side to ranching. A person either loved the land or didn't. Could Amy *learn* to appreciate the wide-open freedom of the Rocking B?

When he'd been dating a variety of women, he

didn't give a rip what they thought of ranch life. But now, everything had changed. No doubt about it, finding a wife was very complicated, and very frustrating.

Blue finished the preparations for breakfast, placing eggs and bacon on a platter in case Amy changed her mind about eating. He carried plates, napkins and silverware to the table, followed by a stack of toast, then two mugs of steaming coffee.

"Your lifesaving brew, ma'am," he said, putting a mug in front of Amy. He sat down opposite her. "Hello?"

Amy jerked upward and blinked.

"Oh! Sorry," she said. "I guess I dozed off. Ah, coffee." She took a sip from the mug and smiled. "Thank you, Blue."

A man would have to be certifiably insane if he didn't appreciate the sight of this pretty woman sitting across from him at the breakfast table, Blue thought. *Smiling* at him.

Man, Amy was so pretty, so fresh and wholesome appearing. She reminded him of a spring day after a soft rain. And the heat low in his body kicked up another notch.

Blue filled his plate from the platter.

"Help yourself," he said.

Amy took a piece of toast and nibbled on a corner of it.

"Sleep well?" Blue asked.

No, Amy thought. She'd been too busy dealing

with the memories of the kiss shared with Blue, and the complexities of Blue Bishop the man.

"Like a rock," she said brightly. "How about you?"

Not even close, Blue thought.

"A rancher usually sleeps like the dead, because he has put in a hard day. I'm sure your readers will be thrilled to know that."

Amy cocked her head to one side as she looked at him.

"You really think my doing this column is nonsense, don't you?" she said.

"No, not totally. I've read some of your columns. The occupations you've covered over the past months have been interesting and informative. It's just that..." He shook his head and took a big bite of toast.

"What, Blue? It's just that what?"

He sipped some coffee, then looked directly at her.

"I'm sure the story about your week here will be as fascinating as the others you've done, Amy. The thing is, being a rancher isn't an occupation, it's a way of life, something that takes devotion and attention twenty-four hours a day, if need be. It's a love of the land, the connection between man and nature.

"Think of it like this, Amy. You could do a column on the week in the life of a mother of a baby. You'd tell about the chores of feeding the infant, bathing it, changing diapers, getting up in the night if the baby cried, the whole nine yards. Are you with me here?''

Amy nodded, her gaze riveted on Blue's face.

He leaned slightly toward her.

''What you would have on paper,'' he went on, ''would be the ongoing duties and responsibilities of that mother. What I'm not certain you could capture would be the *emotions* involved, the indescribable love she has for that child, the depth and intensity of it.

''That, Amy, is how a rancher has to feel about his land. It's his mistress, his child, his life, because when it needs something, it generally can't wait.'' He paused. ''A rancher's wife has to understand and accept that. It doesn't mean she's loved any less than a city wife, she just doesn't always get to be first with her husband. It takes a...well, a rare and special kind of woman to handle that.''

She was going to cry, Amy thought incredulously. There was an ache in her throat and a stinging sensation at the back of her eyes that announced she was a breath away from bursting into tears. She'd been so touched, so deeply moved, by what Blue had just said.

There had been such emotion ringing in his voice, such sincerity and truth. And there had also been a hint of...of franticness, as though he was trying so desperately to make her understand, yet somehow knowing she couldn't.

But she did!

Yes, of course she did, because that type of focus and dedication was how she felt about *her* career choice.

Becoming the best possible journalist she could be required many sacrifices on her part. Her writing was her lover, her child, her life, just as Blue had described what the Rocking B was to him.

Such depths there were to Blue Bishop, so many layers. When he chose that special and rare woman he'd spoken of to be his wife, she would be a very lucky lady.

"I understand what you're saying, Blue, about how you feel about this ranch, the land, what it requires of you. I really do."

"You do?" he asked, his heart beginning to beat faster. "Are you sure?"

"Absolutely."

Amy drained her mug, then rose and crossed the room to the counter for a refill from the pot.

Blue watched her, his mind racing.

Amy had grasped what he was trying to say? In one shot, she'd gotten it? What was her inner reaction to the fact that a rancher's wife often had to take second seat to the land?

Well, there was only one way to find out. Ask her.

When Amy sat back down, Blue cleared his throat.

"So!" he said. "You understood what I was trying to say. That's good. Great, actually. But just out of curiosity, how would you, as a woman, feel about coming in second in my life to a downed fence or a sick horse? Hypothetically speaking, of course.''

"I would have known the facts before I married you...hypothetically...and would believe in the love we share, what we have together.

"Part of my responsibility as your wife would be to understand, accept and support you in your life's choice of a career. There wouldn't be room in our relationship for petty jealousy on my part about the demands of the ranch. That kind of jealousy would destroy us.''

Amy nodded.

"You're right, Blue, it would take a rare and special kind of woman to be your...a rancher's wife. I don't think you'll find one of those around every corner.''

"That's the truth,'' he said. He drained his mug and thudded it onto the table. "How is it you understood me so completely, so quickly? The last woman I tried to explain all this to stared at me and said 'Huh?'''

Amy shrugged. "I guess it's because we're on the same wavelength.''

What! Blue thought, nearly surging to his feet. He was going to leap over the table and take Amy into his arms.

"I feel the same way about *my* career,'' Amy said.

"What?'' Blue felt as though he'd suddenly been doused with a bucket of ice-cold water. "I beg your pardon?''

"It's very simple, Blue." Amy picked up her piece of toast, frowned at it, then dropped it back onto the plate. She looked at Blue again. "I have the same dedication about my chosen life work as you do. Nothing, and no one, will keep me from achieving my goal of being a top-notch journalist."

"But—"

"However," she continued, pointing one finger in the air, "there *is* one major difference in our outlooks."

Blue sighed. "Which is?"

"Well, you feel you can marry and have a family, providing you find the rare and special woman you spoke of."

"Yes."

"I, on the other hand, firmly believe that I can never get married, be a wife and mother. To attempt to have that many roles, wear all those hats, means I would be first-rate at nothing. Everything I did would fall short of excellence because I would be spreading myself too thin."

Blue smacked the table with the palm of one hand. Amy jumped in her chair at his sudden outburst.

"That's nuts," he said, nearly yelling. "Millions of women have families and careers. More than millions."

"Not *this* woman," Amy said, matching his volume. "I've given all this a tremendous amount of thought, and I've made up my mind. I fully intend to concentrate totally on my career. I don't have room in my life for a husband and babies.''

Well, hell, Blue thought, sinking back in his chair. Talk about a rotten attitude. Amy Madison just won the prize in the lousy-mind-set category.

So, Bishop, chalk it up. Amy was no longer a candidate for his wife. Not even close. He'd struck out again, damn it all.

Amy got to her feet and carried her mug and plate to the sink, rinsed them, then placed them in the dishwasher. As she began to wipe off the countertops, Blue crossed his arms over his chest and glowered at the wall, Amy's depressing words echoing in his brain.

Suddenly the remembrance of the kiss shared with Amy slammed into his mind. Heat rocketed throughout him, settling low, hot and coiled.

He could feel, as though it were really happening, the ecstasy of Amy's slender, womanly body nestled against him.

He could taste her sweet mouth, smell her flowery cologne.

And he could feel her respond to his kiss, give of herself, surrender to her desire for him.

He could hear Amy's lilting laughter, see her dark eyes sparkle with merriment.

He'd sat across the table from Amy Madison at dinner the night before and now at breakfast this morning. She looked...*right* sitting in his kitchen, moving around his home.

Blue slid a glance at Amy where she stood at the sink rinsing out the dishcloth.

If he had half a brain, he thought, he would scratch Amy off his wife-candidate list and continue his search elsewhere. There was a very good chance that he would have to do exactly that.

But not yet.

No, sir, he wasn't beaten yet. Something different, and possibly very important, had happened when he'd held Amy in his arms and kissed her, and he had every intention of discovering what it was.

So, okay, Amy had an attitude and outlook so far from wifedom and motherhooddom it was a crime. But attitudes and outlooks could be changed.

Plus, he did *not* like to be dictated to. He would give up on Amy Madison when *he* decided she was a hopeless case in his quest for a wife. The pretty, feisty, delicate lady wasn't telling *him* what to do.

"Don't you like kids?" he asked.

"Oh, yes, I adore them," Amy said, drying her hands on a paper towel. "I wish I had brothers and sisters so I could at least be a doting aunt. But—" she shrugged "—I can't have everything, and I'm fully prepared to make the sacrifices necessary to achieve my career goals." She paused. "Why are we still dwelling on this subject?"

Blue smiled. "It just happens to be what we're talking about." Amy loved babies. Yes! "We're chatting over breakfast, that's all."

Amy returned to the table and sat down.

''Well, let's chat about what you're going to do today. What's on the work agenda for the ranch?''

Before Blue could reply, a loud knock sounded from the back door beyond the mud room.

''Yeah!'' Blue hollered.

''Oh, good grief,'' Amy said, covering her ears.

Moments later, Tink entered the kitchen.

''Mornin', boss,'' he said. ''Ma'am.''

''Tink, I didn't introduce you yesterday,'' Blue said. ''This is Amy Madison, a reporter from the *Holler*. She's doing a story on what it's like to be a Texas rancher.''

''Chaps told us guys,'' Tink said, nodding. ''Feel free to use my name in your column, Ms. Madison. I'd like that just fine.''

Amy smiled. ''Call me Amy.''

''Amy, then,'' Tink said. ''Blue, I was wondering if I could tinker with that car out front in my off time. I was looking it over, and it's in a world of hurt.'' He rubbed his hands together. ''I'm just itching to get my paws on that baby.''

Blue chuckled. ''Amy? It's your car, so it's up to you. I can vouch for Tink's expertise, though.''

''Go for it,'' Amy said, laughing. ''That car is gasping its last breath, I'm afraid. Anything you could do to postpone its demise would be greatly appreciated, Tink.''

''Aw right,'' he said, beaming.

''Are we ready to roll?'' Blue asked.

"Just about," Tink answered. "Chaps is loading the stuff in the wagon now."

"Okay." Blue got to his feet. "I'll meet you at the barn in a few minutes. I want to do that last hundred head. Tell the boys to gear up for a long, hard day."

"Yep." Tink looked at Amy and touched the fingers of one hand to the brim of his Stetson. "Pleasure, ma'am." He spun around and strode out of the kitchen.

"What are you going to do to the last hundred head?" Amy asked Blue. "I assume you're referring to cattle."

Blue nodded. "We're giving them vitamin-A shots. Winter grass has matured beyond having enough vitamin A. So we give the cattle shots."

"Amazing," Amy said. "That's really interesting." She got to her feet, too. "I'll go get my recorder and notebook. Be right back."

"Amy, wait a minute," Blue said, running one hand over the back of his neck. "Why don't I just tell you how this is done? It's a lot of hours of hard, dusty, hot work. You don't want to be out there for this."

Amy lifted her chin. "I most certainly do. This is obviously an important part of tending properly to cattle, and I'm going to witness the event."

"Lord, you're stubborn," Blue said. "Okay, we'll compromise. You come along, and when you've had enough, I'll bring you back to the house."

"But—"

"Compromise is a fantastic invention, Amy. You'd be surprised at what can be accomplished when two people make up their minds to compromise on issues they're dealing with together."

"Thank you for the sermonette," Amy said dryly.

Blue grinned. "You're welcome. It's certainly worth thinking about, isn't it?"

"Right," she said slowly, eyeing him warily. "You're weird sometimes, Blue Bishop."

"Me?" he said, raising his eyebrows. "No way. Look, let's do an exercise in compromise, sort of like show-and-tell, so I can prove my point."

"Your cows are waiting to get a shot in the posterior, or wherever."

"They're cattle, and they're not going to leave town. Are you with me here?"

Amy rolled her eyes heavenward. "All right, Blue, we'll have a show-and-tell demonstration of compromise. What is it going to be? You'll clear the table and I'll load the dishwasher?"

Blue closed the short distance between them, cradled Amy's face in his hands and dipped his head to speak close to her lips.

"No, we're not dealing with the kitchen. I want to kiss you...two, four, ten, twenty kisses," he said, his voice low as he looked directly into her widened-with-shock eyes. "But I'll compromise and settle for one kiss...for now."

"I—"

Blue's mouth melted over Amy's, and whatever she had been about to say was forgotten.

Compromise, her mind echoed hazily. Oh, yes, there were definitely some very positive aspects to compromise. It had been too long, an eternity, since the last kiss shared with Blue.

Amy wrapped her arms around Blue, splaying her hands on his back, savoring the feel of the taut muscles beneath her palms. Her tongue dueled with Blue's, stroking, dancing, heightening her passion to a fever pitch.

A soft purr whispered in Amy's throat.

A groan of need rumbled in Blue's chest.

Time lost meaning as the kiss went on and on.

Then slowly, so reluctantly, Blue broke the kiss and raised his head, his breathing rough. He grasped Amy's shoulders gently, and eased her away from his aroused body.

"So, Ms. Madison," he said, his voice gritty, "*now* what is your opinion of compromise?"

"I think," she said dreamily, "that it's wonderful."

Chapter Six

Amy leaned her head back against the cottonwood tree and sighed with contentment. A cool breeze whispered through the trees, rippling the water in the small man-made pond.

In the distance, she could see Blue and the men busily at work, giving the vitamin shots to the protesting, bellowing cattle. A huge cloud of dust hovered over the area where the operation was taking place. The sounds reaching her were muted, as though she were watching a movie with the volume on low.

For the first two hours on the range, she'd perched next to Chaps on the seat of the wagon, closely observing the wild, noisy procedure. She held the recorder close to her mouth, explaining what she was witnessing.

The men worked in harmony, like a carefully choreographed dance, where each knew his part and performed it with expertise. There were also two dogs as part of the crew. One nipped at the rear legs of a steer to turn it in the direction it should go, while the other dog concentrated on the steer's nose.

Blue twirled a rope high in the air as he approached a steer, then dropped it over the animal's head, instantly yanking it tight as his horse came to a jarring halt.

Tink and a cowboy named Ricky hustled forward to pull the feet out from beneath the steer, then whipped short ropes around the hooves. The last man, Joe, injected the vitamin into the neck of the animal with an enormous needle, then slapped a red paper circle about four inches across on the beast's head.

The paper would dissolve in the first rain they had, Chaps explained to Amy, but for now the bright circle made it clear which animals had received the shot.

When Chaps announced he was heading back to the bunkhouse to make sandwiches to bring out to the crew later, Amy said she would stay behind in the beckoning cove of trees.

She'd settled onto the thick grass, replayed the information she'd recorded and nodded in satisfaction at her detailed report. Then she'd allowed herself to relax, and her mind to drift.

Blue Bishop, she mused, was spellbinding to watch as he moved as one with his gleaming horse. He was...well, poetry in motion, as corny as that sounded, as he twirled the rope above his head, then leaned forward in the saddle to drop the rope and capture his prey. Blue was so powerful, yet so graceful, his body totally under his command.

He was magnificent.

Compromise, Amy's mind suddenly echoed, causing her to frown.

Blue's show-and-tell demonstration of compromise in the kitchen had resulted in them *sharing* another kiss. A kiss that had been even more heated, more sensually intense, than the first one.

"Oh, dear," Amy said aloud.

She had responded *again* in total abandon to Blue's kiss and touch. She'd *wanted* to kiss him, and savored every desire-evoking moment. The really unsettling fact was that she knew that if Blue marched up to her now, took her into his arms and kissed her, she would surrender yet again to the ecstasy.

Compromise.

She had very little experience dealing with the premise, she realized. She'd decided on the course for her life and had moved steadily forward toward her goals and dreams.

But now? Well, due to Gibson McKinley's dictate that she produce two columns a month for the *Holler,* she was having to *compromise* on the way she had previously been producing her stories.

Compromise.

She was failing miserably in her determination to erect a barrier between herself and Blue. The attraction between them was stronger than her willpower to resist it.

Perhaps it was time to grow up, be a bit more worldly, she decided. Everyone around her had been nagging at her, telling her she needed a life beyond her work at the newspaper.

Amy sighed, pressed her fingertips to her temples, then dropped her hands heavily into her lap.

She was so terribly confused and she hated, *really hated*, being terribly confused. She prided herself on her organization, on knowing what she was doing and why she was doing it. All that flew out the window when she was in close proximity to Blue Bishop.

She didn't know why she melted like ice cream in the sun when Blue touched her, or even looked at her with those incredible blue eyes of his.

She didn't know why his kiss was like none before, causing her to want him with a need and intensity that was shocking.

She didn't know why she was behaving like a stranger, both frightening and exciting herself in the same breathless moment.

Oh, dear heaven, it truly was terribly confusing.

But if she *compromised*, accepted her actions and

reactions to Blue as simply the way it was for the duration of her stay at the Rocking B, she wouldn't have to endure the depleting state of confusion.

As long as she knew, remembered at all times, that when she left the ranch at the completion of her assignment, she would never see Blue again, couldn't she compromise on her behavior while there?

"Yes," she said decisively.

Nothing had really changed. She still intended to focus totally on her career. She could not, would not, entertain the idea of marriage and children. Her views on the subject were solidly in place, etched in stone.

But while at the Rocking B, she was going to, as Blue had said, do what felt natural and right. No one would be hurt. She knew the boundaries, the limits, of whatever might transpire between her and Blue.

And Blue? Heavens, the man could have his pick of any woman in the state of Texas. He would forget her before the dust had settled from her driving away from the ranch in her clunky old car.

There. She'd covered the details, organized the situation, created order from muddled confusion.

She should be feeling satisfied and pleased with herself. So why was she registering a sense of near-depression as she envisioned leaving the Rocking B, watching it, and Blue, disappear forever in the distance?

"Forget it," she said, flipping one hand in the air.

"I'm new at this compromise business, that's all. I'll get the hang of it."

Amy's attention was caught by the return of Chaps. A few minutes later, the men were standing by the wagon. Everyone except Blue remounted and galloped off in the opposite direction from where Amy sat. Chaps clucked to the horses pulling the wagon and followed the crew as Blue rode toward Amy.

At the edge of the water hole, Blue swung off his horse. The animal dipped his head into the sparkling water. Blue strode toward Amy, a rolled grocery sack in one hand. He stopped ten feet in front of her and smiled.

"I think I'd better toss you a sandwich from here," he said. "I am one very sweaty, dirty cowboy."

"I'll survive," Amy said, laughing. She patted the grass. "Come where it's cool."

Blue settled next to her, placing his Stetson on the ground, then pulled off heavy gloves.

"At least my hands are clean," he said. "Whew. I'm definitely ready for a break." He opened the sack and gave Amy a sandwich wrapped in wax paper, a can of soda and an orange. "A gourmet lunch, ma'am. Nothing but the best on the Rocking B."

Amy managed to mumble a thank-you as she stared at Blue. Her heart was beating so rapidly, she had the irrational thought that he surely could hear the wild tempo.

Blue Bishop sat with his shirt plastered by perspiration to his broad chest and back, his face streaked with dust that was closer to being plain old mud. He looked as if he needed to be hosed down, clothes and all.

And the sight of him was causing heat to lick throughout her, hotter and hotter with every beat of her racing heart.

There was a magnificent earthy aura emanating from Blue, a raw male essence that was overwhelming her. He was so real, so alive, so vibrantly male.

Blue was talking to her, she realized hazily. He was chattering away about how well the work had gone so far, the fact that they were ahead of schedule in the number of cattle having been given the vitamin-A shots and something about storm clouds building on the horizon.

Amy half listened, even nodded and commented in appropriate places, but she felt as though she were floating above herself, watching, hearing, from afar.

She was acutely aware, not only of Blue, but of herself, as well. Her skin was tingling, her breasts were heavy, achy, her femininity, deep and low and dark, was throbbing with a foreign pulse.

She was earthy, real, alive and vibrantly *female*. She was Blue's counterpart. She was a woman, and she gloried in that fact as she absorbed every nuance, gesture, the aroma, the sight, of Blue Bishop.

Oh, dear heaven, she thought frantically, she

wanted to run as far and as fast as she could. She had to get away from this strange spell Blue was casting over her.

No, she wanted to stay close to him, savor the sensuous sensations consuming her, cherish them, memorize every detail, etch it all indelibly in her mind and...heart?

"Okay?" Blue said.

Amy blinked, her thoughts fragmented.

"Pardon me?" she said in a near-whisper.

"Am I boring you?" he said, grinning.

"No, of course not. I...I was digesting everything you've said. I just missed the last part."

"I said the boys have gone about a mile over to a larger watering spot. Even as we speak, they're skinny-dipping to cool off. Chaps will collect the debris from lunch, then stop back by here. I suggest that you go with him to the house. The rest of the day will be more of what you've seen."

"Yes," she said, nodding. "That's fine. I'll go with Chaps when he comes."

Blue frowned. "Amy, is something wrong? Are you feeling all right?"

"Yes," she said quickly. She took a bite of what proved to be a ham sandwich, chewed, and swallowed. "I'm hungry, that's all. Mmm. Delicious."

"You're positive you're okay?"

Amy took another bite, then forced herself to smile as she nodded.

Blue studied her for a long moment, then polished

off his sandwich and reached in the sack for another one.

"Do your parents live in Houston?" he asked, handing her a paper towel. "Hey, I see the frown starting. Let's be fair here. You're learning everything there is to know about me, including what I had for breakfast. Can't you talk a bit about yourself?"

"I'm gathering data on you for my column."

Blue took a drink of soda, then glared at her.

"Come on, Amy," he said, a slight edge to his voice. "I'd hate to think that the kisses we've shared have been research for your story."

"Don't be absurd. Those kisses have nothing to do with my column. Do you believe I kiss all the subjects of my stories? That's really insulting."

"No, I *don't* think that. That's the point I'm trying to make. Look, it doesn't take a genius to realize that you're a dedicated journalist. Not only have you said as much, but I can tell by the way you've tackled this assignment from the moment you arrived here."

Amy smiled. "I'm cheating. I have a stash of library books under my bed because Gibson McKinley didn't allow me enough time to do research." She shrugged.

Blue chuckled. "Your secret is safe with me." His smile faded. "I'd like to know more about *you*, the person, the woman."

"Why?"

"Because that's who I've been kissing, damn it!"

Amy blinked in surprise at Blue's outburst.

"Oh," she said, "I see."

"Do you?" He nodded sharply. "Good. Okay, then, talk to me. Who are you, Amy Madison?"

Amy opened her mouth, shut it, frowned, then tried again.

"There isn't much to tell you, now that I really think about it, Blue. I was born, I grew up, went to college, am now a journalist for the *Houston Holler*.

"I'm an only child. My father died of an unexpected heart attack five years ago, and I still miss him. He was a corporate attorney.

"My mother, Margaret Madison, is wonderful, and we're very close. She's financially secure, due to my father's loving and intelligent planning, so she donates her time teaching piano to underprivileged children."

Amy paused.

"That's it," she said. "End of story."

"Hooray for the résumé about your parents," Blue said, glaring at her.

Amy threw out her arms, nearly smacking him with her sandwich.

"What do you want from me, Blue? I work. Okay? What more is there to say, for Pete's sake?"

Blue sighed. "Ah, Amy, what are you afraid of? You've got a solid wall built around yourself that might have a door, but you're sure as hell hiding the key."

He drew one thumb gently over her lips. Amy shivered from the feathery touch.

"What's your favorite color?" Blue said, looking directly into her eyes, his voice low. "What kind of books do you read for pleasure? Do you cry when you watch sad, or romantic, movies? What do you feel, inside, when you stand perfectly still and witness the beauty, the miracle, of a Texas dawn?"

"I..." Amy had to stop and take a breath because she realized she'd been hardly breathing as she'd listened to Blue's questions. "I've never discussed things like that with anyone."

"Then it's time. I'm the 'anyone,' and I'm listening. Please?"

"Well, um, my favorite color is peach...soft, warm peach. I read mysteries when I have time, and cheer for myself when I figure out who did it before the end of the book. Do I cry while watching movies? Heavens, I cry during greeting-card commercials on television. But I guess...I guess I've never stopped long enough to really look at a Texas dawn."

Amy tore her eyes from Blue's and picked bits of crust from her sandwich. She felt strange, vulnerable, stripped as bare as if she'd just whipped off all her clothes and skipped down a busy Houston street.

"Amy, look at me," Blue said quietly.

She turned her head slowly to meet his gaze. He slid one hand to the nape of her neck.

"Thank you," he said, beginning to lower his

head toward hers. "I'll cherish what you just shared with me, I really will."

And then he kissed her; so softly, gently, so reverently, that a sob caught in Amy's throat and tears misted her eyes.

Blue lifted his head before Amy could totally respond to the kiss, wanting it that way, wanting to give the kiss to her as a gesture of gratitude, asking nothing in return. He straightened, putting undesired distance between them, then smiled at her warmly.

Two tears slid down Amy's cheeks. She dropped her sandwich and dashed the tears away with an angry, jerky motion. In the next instant, she scrambled to her feet, wrapping her hands around her elbows. She looked at Blue, took one step backward, then another.

"Darn you, Blue Bishop," she said, her voice quavering. "Just when I'm convinced that I have everything figured out about how to handle this...this whatever it is between us, you throw me a curve by doing something so unexpected, so...so special, so damnably *nice*, that you muddle me up again, confusing me to the point that I can't even think."

"Me?" he said. He raised his eyebrows, an expression of total innocence on his face. "*I* do that?"

"Yes! You! I want you to just knock it off. Do you hear me? I..."

Amy paused, drew a wobbly breath, then sighed as she dropped her arms heavily to her sides.

"This is great, just wonderful," she said, shaking

her head. "I'm throwing a tantrum. What's next? I stamp my foot and stick out my tongue at you? You're driving me absolutely nuts, Blue, that's what you're doing."

Blue rolled to his feet, closed the distance between them and grasped her shoulders.

"Why? Why am I making you crazy, Amy? Because I'm *seeing* you as a woman, as well as a journalist? *Treating* you as a woman, as well as a journalist? Well, color me guilty if those are the charges against me, because you *are* both, and I'm very aware of that fact.

"*You* decided how to deal with what's happening between us?" he continued. "Aren't you forgetting something? The key word there is *us*. Just how did you plan to *handle* this?"

"I don't wish to discuss it," she said, staring at a pearly snap on his Western shirt.

"That's not fair," he said, his voice gaining volume. "I'm the other half of the *us*."

Amy's head snapped up, and anger sparked in the dark pools of her big eyes.

"Okay, okay," she said. "First, I decided to keep my distance from you, concentrate on my assignment for the newspaper and ignore the strange pull that kept weaving around us, but then... Oh, drat."

"Then?" Blue prompted.

"I couldn't do it," she went on, nearly yelling. "There I was, *sharing* another kiss with you, wanting it, wanting...you. So I regrouped, organized my thoughts, redid my mind-set and decided I'd just do what felt natural and right...as a journalist and, yes, as a woman."

"Perfect," Blue said, smiling. He dropped his hands from her shoulders. "Fantastic."

"It is not! Making that decision still allowed me to be in charge, in control, of *me*." She splayed one hand on her chest. "Do you understand what I'm saying?

"But then, you rotten, sneaky bum, you somehow managed to get me to tell you that my favorite color is soft, warm peach, and made me wish I'd stopped long enough to enjoy the beauty of a Texas dawn.

"I don't have time to stand around sighing over Texas dawns and sunsets, Blue. I have a career that needs my total concentration. Are you getting this?"

Blue stared at Amy for a long, silent moment, with no readable expression. He squinted at the sky, the toe of one boot, then looked at her again.

"'Rotten, sneaky bum'?" he finally said, a grin breaking across his face.

"That does it," Amy said, stomping around him. "That's it. You're infuriating, Blue Bishop, you really are." She snatched her sandwich from the ground, frowned at it, then dumped it in the sack. "You've scrambled my brain, and I don't appreciate it, not one iota. From now on... Oh, just forget it."

Blue walked slowly to where she stood.

"From now on...what?" he said quietly. He looked directly into her eyes, pinning her in place.

"Forget what you feel when we share a kiss? Forget the hot, burning desire that threatens to send you up in flames? Forget that you told me only a few minutes ago that you want those kisses, that you *want* me?"

"Stop it," she whispered.

"How are you going to do that, Amy? I know I can't...forget it, any of it. Oh, I want you, too, Amy Madison. I want to make slow, sweet love to you all through the night, over and over again, until we're sated, exhausted, contented.

"Then I'll take your hand, lead you outside, and there we'll stand, not speaking, just savoring, the miracle of a beautiful Texas dawn.

"And, Amy, all of it...*all of it*...will be natural and right, for both of us."

"Blue, please," she said, tears threatening once again, "don't, just don't."

He lifted one hand and cradled the softness of her cheek, warmth and tenderness radiating from his sapphire blue eyes. Amy's breath caught on a sob.

"Natural and right," he repeated, stroking her cheek with his thumb in a slow, steady rhythm. "But unless you believe that, really believe it, nothing more is going to happen. What I'm saying is, it will be up to you."

Amy's eyes widened and she moved her head, forcing Blue to drop his hand, to stop the tantalizing caress of her cheek so she might, hopefully, be able to think straight.

"Up to me?" she said. "You can't place the responsibility for something like...like we do, or don't, make love, entirely on my shoulders."

"I have to, because I already know that it would be natural and right for me. There's something different going on between us, Amy, that isn't quite like anything I've experienced before. I don't know what it is, but I sure as hell intend to find out."

"But—"

"Because I *don't* know what it is, and there's a chance it might be very important, very special, I'm not gumming up the works by trying to seduce you."

Blue smiled. "Nope, I'm going to sit back and wait for you to come to me. As the old saying goes, the ball, ma'am, is in your court. When you're ready to make love with me, I'll be one very happy cowboy."

"When? When! Have you ever considered the possibility of 'if,' Blue Bishop? You're getting cocky and arrogant again. Do you honestly believe that it's just a matter of time before I leap into your bed? Well...well...ha!"

Blue walked to where his Stetson lay on the grass, picked it up, settled it onto his head, then tugged it low in front.

"Whatever you say, ma'am," he said pleasantly.

"I mean it, Blue," Amy said, planting her hands on her hips. "We are *not* going to make love."

"Mmm."

Blue began to pick up the debris from lunch, placing it in the sack.

Amy hurried to stand next to him where he was tending to the chore.

"I know that I said I desired you, wanted you," she rattled on, "but that doesn't mean for one second that I intend to do anything about the fact that I... Not on your life, buster."

"Yes, ma'am."

"Quit calling me 'ma'am'!"

Blue straightened and grinned at her. "My mother raised me to be polite...ma'am."

"Your mother deserves a medal of valor for having *survived* raising you."

"You know, you're probably right," he said thoughtfully, "especially when you consider the fact that there were three of us. Yep, the Bishop boys, Tux, Blue and Bram, that's us."

"Forget valor," she said crossly. "Your mother is eligible for sainthood."

Blue hooted with laughter, then sobered in the next moment as he glanced beyond Amy.

"The boys are back," he said. "Chaps is headed this way to take you to the house." He looked at Amy. "We understand each other, right?"

"Pardon me?"

"Amy, Amy, maybe you should have taken notes like you do for the stories for the *Holler.* Okay, short and sweet. Here it is. I want to make love with you. You want to make love with me.

"However, because this is not basic lust, but something presently undefinable, it must be treated with the utmost respect until everything feels natural and right.

"I'm already there. I'll wait until you reach that place, too, with no rotten-sneaky-bum attempts at seduction. Your call, your ball. Think about it." He leaned down and brushed his lips over hers. "Ma'am."

Chapter Seven

After showering and washing her hair, Amy once again tackled the kitchen, which was in disarray from Blue's breakfast endeavor.

She defrosted a small pork roast, surrounded it with peeled potatoes, then pushed the baking pan into the oven.

The cupboards produced cake and frosting mixes, and she set about making a chocolate cake that would boast maple frosting.

She was not, Amy told herself, being domestic. Heaven forbid. Nor was she enjoying the challenge of applying her journalistic organization skills to a household arena.

No, this time she performed the chores to enable

herself to focus somewhere other than on the muddled mess in her mind. She would clean, cook, bake. She would *not* think.

She slid the two round pans of cake batter onto the rack above the roast, then closed the oven door with a nod of satisfaction. As she straightened, she stared up at the ceiling as she heard a sudden, loud, rolling rumble of thunder.

She glanced out the window over the sink to see the sky darkening as storm clouds swept rapidly in from the horizon.

Winter storms were common in Houston, usually producing torrents of rain, along with a great deal of thunder and lightning. It was not unusual for the electricity to go out, Amy knew, leaving a person without power anywhere from minutes to hours.

To avoid any problems, she found candles and wooden holders on a top shelf in a cabinet and set them on the table with a book of matches. She peeked into the mud room, saw three flashlights on the supply shelving and placed one on the kitchen counter.

Inhaling the delectable aromas of baking pork and chocolate cake, she made a huge tossed salad, covered it in plastic wrap and put the bowl in the refrigerator.

Noting how much time she had before the cake would be done, she wandered through the living room to the room beyond where she'd seen the piano. As she reached for a magazine among those scattered on the coffee table, she noticed an open door that she hadn't previously realized was there on the far wall.

Standing in the doorway to the newly discovered room, Amy nodded instantly in comprehension as to what this area was for. It was an office of sorts, where Blue must spend countless hours tending to the paperwork that was required when operating a working ranch.

She made a mental note to ask Blue questions about ranch record keeping for her article.

"Oh, great," Amy said aloud with a sigh.

She'd been doing so well, just puttering away, keeping her mind blank, having a much-needed reprieve from the havoc Blue Bishop was creating in her once-serene existence. Now she'd brought Blue front-row center with her reminder to interview him about the paperwork part of ranching.

Amy glanced at her watch.

"Cake," she said. "I'm not thinking about Blue. My cake is ready to come out of the oven."

She hurried across the room, heading for the kitchen.

Nearly an hour later, Amy stepped back once again from the counter to squint at the two-layer cake.

It was a disaster, she thought dismally. It was so lopsided, it was a crime.

She'd tried shifting the layers, shoving them this way and that, which hadn't helped one iota.

Her last solution was to shore up one side with great globs of frosting, which had improved the appearance of the creation a tad.

But what she had ultimately created was a very sad example of a two-layer chocolate cake with maple frosting. It looked more like a basketball with half of the air squished out.

A boom of thunder directly over the house caused her to jump. Rain began to fall in sheets, pelting the window as it was whipped by a rising wind.

She gripped the edge of the sink and stood on tiptoe to get as close to the window as possible, hoping to glimpse Blue heading for the house and out of the treacherous storm. All she could see was beating rain and her own reflection against a background of darkness.

Amy sighed and turned, leaning against the counter and crossing her arms beneath her breasts, a frown on her face.

One would think that a supposedly intelligent man like Blue would have enough sense to come in out of the rain. Why was he still out there? Surely they had all seen the storm clouds rolling in and had headed back from the range. Hadn't they? So where was Blue?

Amy began to pace the floor, glancing often at the door leading to the mud room, straining to hear any sound of Blue entering the house above the cacophony of the storm. But all she heard was nature's fury.

The minutes ticked slowly by.

A cold knot of fear began to tighten in her stomach.

Was something wrong? Was someone hurt? Had Blue been injured out there in the midst of the angry cattle that wanted no part of being stuck with a huge needle? Were the other hands now tending to Blue, bringing his crumpled, bleeding body back to the house in a somber procession?

Amy halted her trek and pressed her hands to her pale cheeks.

Stop it, Amy Madison, she admonished herself. She was allowing her imagination to run away with her. There was a perfectly reasonable explanation as to why Blue hadn't yet appeared.

So what if the storm was becoming more vicious by the second, the thunder and lightning more intense? Blue knew that lightning was extremely dangerous on the open range and wouldn't put his life at risk.

So where was he?

She didn't want anything to happen to Blue. She just couldn't bear the thought. The image in her mind of him hurt in some way was horrifying, causing the knot in her stomach to clinch tighter, and the achy sensation in her throat threatened tears.

Oh, Blue, please, her mind whispered, *come home. Come home safe and sound, Blue. Come home...to me.*

Come home to me?

No, no, wait, wait, she thought, flapping her hands

in the air. She hadn't meant that the way it was now echoing over and over in her head.

Blue Bishop should be warm, dry and safe inside the house like a sensible human being. She just happened to be in said house. Therefore, her frazzled and frantic brain had erroneously connected the two facts, thus producing the ridiculous plea *come home to me.*

That made sense, didn't it? Oh, she couldn't think straight. She was just so worried about Blue that everything else was a mishmash of confusion.

A sudden noise brought Amy from her jumbled thoughts. She rushed to the door leading to the mud room and flung it open.

Across the mud room by the door, dripping wet and very muddy, stood Blue. Alive. Apparently unhurt. Water, not blood, was pooling at his booted feet.

A rush of relief swept over Amy as she decided vaguely that Blue was the most gorgeous, drenched, grungy man she had ever seen.

He was home. He was safe. Oh, thank God, he was all right.

Amy opened her mouth to tell him how glad she was to see him, how concerned she'd been, how grateful she was that he was standing there where she could look at him.

But instead, she heard herself yell, "Blue Bishop, where in heaven's name have you been?"

Oh, mercy, she thought, from out of nowhere had

come a shrieking shrew who had taken over her body
and, even worse, her mouth.

It was too much, it really was. The whole day had
been too long, too emotionally confusing and drain-
ing, and had been topped off by the heartfelt worry
over Blue being out in the raging storm.

She just couldn't handle any more of this.

And with that defeated conclusion, Amy Madison
burst into tears.

Blue stood statue still, staring at Amy as though
he'd never seen her before in his life.

He forgot that he was bone weary, wet to the skin
and hungry.

He forgot that he was freezing cold, because a
warmth was suffusing him from head to toe.

Amy Madison, he thought jubilantly, cared. He
knew she did, because she was obviously a worried
wreck about him having been out in the storm so
long.

Bishop, get a grip, he told himself in the next instant. He had a weeping woman on his hands, one
who was crying because of jangled nerves regarding
his safety. Wasn't that something? Yeah, well, he
had to handle this right, respond to Amy's reactions
in the proper manner, or he would screw this up roy-
ally.

He sure wished he could put Amy and her tears
on hold long enough to go telephone Bram or Tux
and ask for some advice.

You're on your own, Bishop. Don't blow it.

He plunked his Stetson on the hat rack, then removed his boots and socks as quickly as he could. Still dripping water in a steady plunk-plunk, he crossed the room to where Amy stood in the doorway to the kitchen. She had covered her face with her hands and was crying softly.

Blue raised one hand, decided he didn't know quite what to do with it and dropped it back to his side.

"Amy," he said quietly, "I'm very sorry I upset you by staying out in the storm so long."

Amy sniffled, but kept her head bent and her face covered with her hands.

"We saw the storm rolling in," Blue went on, "but we had to finish the inoculations. There were about a dozen head of cattle left to do, and we had to cut them out of the bunch and keep them separated. We had no choice but to stay put, because once the rain started—"

Amy's head popped up.

"The red paper circles on the cattle that had received the shots already would have dissolved in the rain," she said in a rush of words, "and you wouldn't know which ones were done and which weren't. Right?"

Blue smiled. "Right."

Amy dashed the tears from her cheeks.

"That makes perfect sense," she said. "Oh, Blue, I'm so sorry I screamed at you like that. I didn't *plan* to holler. I just opened my mouth, and out it came. I really do apologize.''

Blue placed one wet hand on Amy's tear-dampened cheek.

"No apology is necessary," he said, looking directly into her eyes. That bellowing of Amy's had been music to his ears. Because he now knew that she cared enough about him to be very worried about his welfare. And that felt good. "Something sure smells great."

"Dinner. I forgot all about it. It should be more than ready to be served up and eaten."

"I'll go take a quick shower and put on dry clothes." Blue paused. "Amy?" He brushed his lips over hers. "Thank you."

Amy laughed. "For screaming at you?"

"Bingo," he said.

Amy stepped back so Blue could head for his bedroom. She watched him leave the kitchen, then drew a steadying breath.

Well, Ms. Madison, she thought dryly, *that was quite a performance you put on.*

Shaking her head in self-disgust, she hurried to turn off the oven and remove the roasting pan. As she busied herself getting the meal on the table, her mind lingered time and again on Blue's gently spoken thank-you.

Weird, she mused, setting two glasses of milk in place. She'd hollered her head off, and the recipient of the screaming meemies *thanked* her for the unreasonable tirade? Why had Blue done that? Men were very complicated creatures; that was for certain.

Once everything was on the table, Amy sat down to wait for Blue. Through the entire afternoon, she had managed to ignore what had taken place during lunch with Blue among the cottonwood trees.

But now, unbidden, the memories slammed into her mind and refused to budge.

She heard Blue saying that he wanted to make love with her, and that he knew she desired him.

She heard him state that whatever happened between them must be, would be, natural and right.

And she heard Blue declare that the ultimate decision was hers.

"Drat," she said aloud.

How was she to deal with making such a momentous decision? She alone was responsible for whatever took place between her and Blue.

"I want to go home, "she muttered dismally. "I'm on brain-circuit overload."

She heard Blue whistling a peppy tune in the distance, and straightened in her chair. She practiced a pleasant smile, rejected it, then tried another.

Blue strode into the kitchen and slid onto the chair across from her, rubbing his hands together as he surveyed the culinary offerings.

"This looks delicious," he said. "I'm a starving man. This was really a fantastic thing to do, Amy, fixing dinner again. I appreciate it very much. Now, then, you fill your plate first. What do you want?"

You, Amy thought dreamily. He was wearing a pale blue V-neck sweater with no shirt beneath. The soft material molded enticingly to his broad chest. Moist, dark curls were peeking above the dip at the neckline, beckoning her to entwine her fingers, to play, tantalize, tease and stroke.

"Amy?"

She jumped in her chair. "Salad." She snatched up the bowl. "Veggies are good. Healthy. Of course, tomatoes are a fruit, but fruit is healthy, too, so salad is an all-around healthy—"

"You're babbling," Blue interrupted. "Is something wrong?"

"Oh, no," she said breezily, plopping some salad onto her plate. "It's just been a long and rather stressful day."

"I see," Blue said, accepting the salad bowl she shoved at him. "The storm isn't upsetting you, is it?"

"It upset me while you were still out... there...in..." She shook her head. "No, storms don't frighten me. Would you carve the roast, please?"

It just got better and better, Blue thought rather smugly. The only thing that had disturbed Amy about the wild storm was that he'd been out there in it. Amy was jangled, all right, and it *had* to be because she realized that her feelings for him were growing, slowly but surely.

And *his* feelings for Amy were growing, but there

was nothing *slow* about it. Even in the midst of the backbreaking chore of inoculating bellowing, angry cattle, he'd thought about Amy.

He hadn't even minded getting drenched by the rain, because he'd known that when the work was finished he would be heading for the house where Amy was waiting for him.

But that wasn't all. It was Amy herself, the woman, who caused him to smile at times when it would appear there was absolutely nothing to smile about.

The mere remembrance of the kisses shared with Amy Madison created burning desire that coiled low in his body. He wanted to make love with her with a need that was far beyond anything he'd ever known. Their joining would be natural and right, and beautiful.

Blue frowned as he carved the roast.

He'd told Amy—and he'd meant it—that whatever took place between them was now up to her. He sure as hell didn't like turning over the control of such a major part of his life to someone else, but what choice did he have? What was happening with Amy was special.

So all he could do was wait. All he could do was hope that Amy would allow herself to embrace her feelings for him. But she had such an adamant stand that there was no room in her life for anything but her career. Why did she feel so strongly about that?

Blue placed a slice of the succulent pork roast on

Amy's plate and watched her help herself to one of the crispy, brown potatoes and another serving of salad. Blue filled his plate, and they ate in silence for several minutes, taking the edge off their ravenous appetites.

"Mmm," Blue said finally, "this is scrumptious. You're an excellent cook. Did you learn at your mother's knee?"

Amy laughed. "Relatively speaking. From the time I was three or four years old, my mom would let me stand on a chair next to her in the kitchen when she was cooking and baking. I'd dump stuff in a bowl and beat it to death. I loved it, and in time I learned how to cook a halfway decent meal.

"My efforts at baking always seemed to miss the mark, though. My mother had to give me a lot of it's-the-thought-that-counts speeches for my attempts at baking."

"It sounds as though you had a terrific childhood, just as I did," Blue said. "Imagine that, we're two people who aren't going to point accusing fingers at our parents for gumming up our lives."

"Which is rather rare in this day and age," Amy said, nodding.

"Your mother didn't work outside the house?" Blue said, looking at Amy very closely.

"No, she stayed home to care for me, my dad, our home, but—"

"But?" he prompted.

"Nothing." Amy reached for another slice of meat.

Easy now, Bishop, Blue told himself. He had to come across casual and chatty, like someone taking part in idle conversation over dinner.

"So, your mother is a homemaker," he said, spooning three more potatoes onto his plate. "Was she the person who taught you your theory that a woman can't do justice to more than one role at a time? You know, either have a husband and kids, or a career. Did you learn *that* at your mother's knee?"

"Not exactly," Amy said slowly. "She never sat me down for a serious mother-and-daughter discussion about the subject. In fact, I don't believe she mentioned it at all. Not that I remember anyway."

"Then why do you have such—" Blue paused. Cockeyed? Harebrained? No, he had to come up with something better than that "—*strong* feelings on the subject?"

"One does not always have to be the recipient of a dissertation to enable one to gather accurate data. I know what I know. Facts are facts."

Blue leaned slightly toward her.

"Amy," he said, "did it ever occur to you that you might be wrong?"

"No. This is an arena where your ever-famous compromise simply can't be applied. I will *not* do anything in half measure. By spreading myself too thin over career, wife and mother roles, everyone would suffer the consequences of there not being enough of me to go around. I couldn't live that way, Blue, I just couldn't.''

Damn, Blue thought, he was getting nowhere fast trying to scale that stubborn wall Amy had built around herself on this issue. He was trying, and failing miserably, to make even a dent in her rock-hard beliefs.

Well, he wasn't beaten yet. No sir, Blue Bishop didn't go down for the count without a fight.

''Since you're so focused on being a top-notch journalist,'' he said, still striving for a casual tone of voice, ''did you know since you were a little kid that that was what you wanted to be when you grew up?''

''Like you knew you wanted to be a cowboy since you were six years old?''

''Yeah, like that.''

''Well, no, I actually wanted to... Blue, why are we discussing this?''

He shrugged. ''We're just chatting, like the other times we've been just chatting. You actually wanted to what?''

''Well, from the time I was a little girl and all the way through high school, I wrote children's stories. I imagined myself as an author of wonderful books for children.''

''Sounds good.''

''Not really. It's an extremely difficult market to break into. I...yes, I compromised, and settled on being a journalist. And that, as they say, is that.''

''Interesting,'' Blue said. ''Very interesting.''

"Oh, goodness, I'm stuffed," Amy said, with a moan. "I can't eat another bite. Would you like some cake?"

"Sure." Blue got to his feet. "You cooked, I'll clean. Sit still while I clear the table and put the food away. Then you can produce your cake creation."

Amy raised her eyebrows. "You're going to clean the kitchen?"

"Yep."

"I'll be darned," she said under her breath.

"I heard that," he said, laughing.

When Amy finally placed the lopsided cake on the table, Blue stared at it for a very long moment, then grinned.

"Amy," he said, "it's the thought that counts."

Amy dissolved in a fit of laughter, sinking onto her chair to catch her breath. She waved off Blue's offer of a slice of the cake, then watched as he took a bite of his generous serving.

"Wait," she said suddenly. "You cut the wrong side. All you have there is a big blob of—"

"Frosting," Blue said, then took a drink of milk. "Whew. That was very maple. Yes, sir, *very* maple."

"Whack a piece off the other side. There's cake under there. I promise."

As Blue reached for the knife, a loud boom of thunder sounded directly over the house. Seconds later, the lights flickered, then went out, turning the kitchen into a pitch-black cave.

Chapter Eight

Amy's soft gasp of surprise was accompanied by Blue's much louder expletive at the power outage.

"Well, so be it," Amy said. "I put a flashlight on the counter in case this happened. I'll go get it and—"

"Hold it," Blue interrupted. "I saw candles and matches on the table, didn't I?"

"Yes, but—"

"Sit tight." Blue fumbled around, clanked into the salad bowl, then finally struck a match. He lit each candle in turn and secured them in the wooden holders. "There we go. What do you think?"

What did she think? Amy's mind echoed. That she'd better run for the hills, or hide in a closet. Blue

Bishop, in the glow of romantic candlelight, was unbelievable...and dangerous.

Her heart was beating a wild tattoo, and the heated pulse of desire was thrumming low and so very hot within her that she was unable to tear her gaze from his compelling and incredible sapphire eyes.

Dear heaven, she was in trouble.

Blue looked directly into Amy's big dark eyes, the racing tempo of his heart thundering in his ears.

Flashlights were nice, he thought hazily. He should have gotten up, maneuvered through the darkness to the counter and grabbed the stupid flashlight.

But, no, not Brilliant Bishop. He'd announced that he would just light those handy candles, since they were right there on the table where...*where Amy had put them.* Yes! Amy had searched the cupboards to find candles, when three flashlights were within easy reach in the mud room.

Of course, she couldn't have known the electricity would go out, but she'd been prepared in the event that it did. The candles were at his fingertips. The flashlight was across the room. Interesting.

The seductive aura surrounding them was of Amy's design. All he had to do now was sit back and see what she intended to do next.

He must *not* give way to the desire steadily building within him, hotter and hotter. He must *not* move around the table, haul Amy to her feet and kiss her senseless. He must *not* go up in flames of want and need, and lose touch with reality and reason.

Control, Bishop, he told himself. Get it together. *Keep* it together. It was Amy's call.

Blue rocked his chair onto the two back legs and folded his arms loosely over his chest.

"Well, this is cozy," he said pleasantly. He glanced at the ceiling, then looked at Amy again, savoring the sight of her in the glow of the flickering candlelight. "That storm is really roaring. The electricity is liable to be out for hours."

"My computer is capable of operating on batteries," Amy said. She fiddled with a napkin that Blue had left behind when he'd cleared the table. "I really should work on my article. Yes, that's what I'll do. I'll take a flashlight to my room and get busy."

Amy was getting cold feet, Blue thought. She'd set out the candles on a maybe-they-would-be-needed premise, and now she was bailing out. He'd stated that she could call the shots, but it wouldn't be against the law to nudge her a tad back in the direction she'd originally decided on.

"That would be very hard on your eyes," Blue said. "A concentrated beam like that would definitely cause eyestrain. As for candlelight...well, it's not bright enough. Candles are nice, though. I'm glad you thought to put them out, instead of just stacking up the flashlights."

She *had* searched until she'd found the candles, Amy thought. Looking back, she couldn't remember what she'd been thinking at the time.

And now here she was, in the midst of a situation of her own making, having no idea what to do.

Why wasn't she on her feet, flashlight in hand, heading for her room? That was what she should be doing.

But she didn't want to.

The candlelight was creating a soft, warm, romantic world, where no one existed but Amy Madison and Blue Bishop. The storm was a symphony provided by nature for just the two of them. It was all so lovely, serene, so private, so *natural and right.*

Amy's breath caught.

Natural and right? her mind echoed. Had she been hoping, on a subconscious level, that the electricity would go out, that Blue would light the candles, that the sensuous aura now weaving around them would be created?

Had she set everything in motion so she could follow the dictates of her desire...her heart?

Oh, dear heaven, why didn't she know the answers to the multitude of important and confusing questions?

"Would you like to go into the other room?" Blue said, bringing Amy from her tangled thoughts. "The temperature has dropped at least twenty degrees, and I can make a nice fire in the hearth. It would be a lot more comfortable than sitting on these chairs until the lights come back on."

As though viewing herself from afar, Amy watched as she got to her feet, picked up one of the candle holders, then followed Blue from the room. He carried the other candle, creating a dancing beacon of light.

They crossed the living room to the family room. Amy sat on the floor in front of the fireplace, leaning her back against an oatmeal-colored sofa. Blue made quick work of starting a fire, then settled next to her...close. He blew out the candles, and they both stared at the mesmerizing flames of the fire.

Amy willed her wildly racing heart to quiet, pleaded with her befuddled mind to sift and sort through the jumbled maze.

Slowly, slowly, she calmed, felt herself regain control of the very essence of who she was. The fire crackled, and the leaping orange flames soothed her frazzled nerves. The warring voices of confusion stilled, leaving only a single whispered message.

She wanted to make love with Blue Bishop.

There was no tomorrow.

There was not even the minutes, or hours, ahead until the electricity was restored and with it, reality.

There was only now, the moment, and the want of Blue.

Amy turned her head slowly to look at Blue's rugged profile.

"Blue," she said softly.

Every muscle in Blue's body tensed as he continued to stare straight ahead. The heat from the fire seemed to have suddenly leapt from the hearth to within him with licking flames.

All Amy had said was his name, yet he knew that when he turned his head to meet her gaze he would see desire radiating from the depths of her big brown eyes.

The message had been there in the way she had spoken his name. He'd heard it loud and clear. It was really something to be so connected to a woman, to understand what she was feeling when she'd done nothing more than speak his name.

Blue shifted his eyes from the hearth to Amy's face slowly, wanting to savor the moment, the wonder of it all.

When his eyes met hers, his heart thundered like nature's music in the heavens.

"Ah, Amy."

She smiled at him gently, warmly.

"Are you sure?" he said. "Is it natural—?"

"And right," she finished for him.

They reached for each other at the same time, Amy's arms encircling Blue's neck, his hands splaying on her back. Their lips met in a searing kiss, with tongues stoking the hot flames of desire within them.

Blue raised his head to take a quick, rough breath, then slanted his mouth the other way, drinking in the sweet taste of Amy, inhaling her flowery aroma, relishing the feel of her soft, slender body.

Amy sunk her fingertips into Blue's thick, damp hair, urging his mouth harder onto hers. He tasted like maple frosting, smelled like soap and fresh air, felt like heaven itself.

Blue broke the kiss, rolled to his feet, then extended one hand to Amy, a hand that was not quite steady. She placed her hand in his, and he drew her up, nestling her close as he claimed her mouth once more.

They stepped back and shed their clothes quickly, no longer tolerant of the barriers between them. They stood naked before one another, the firelight casting a rosy glow over a body hard and muscled and aroused, and a body soft and lush and womanly.

Their gazes swept over one another, etching every detail indelibly in their minds, savoring and cherishing it all. Their eyes met. The desire, the earthy passion within them, was there to be seen in its honesty.

"You're so very beautiful, Amy," Blue said, his voice raspy.

"So are you, Blue," she whispered.

It was all so real.

It was all so natural.

It was all *so right*.

They sank to the plush carpeting, Blue stretching out next to Amy and resting on one forearm. He spread his hand on her flat stomach, then moved it upward to gently caress one breast as his mouth melted over hers. His thumb stroked the nipple of her breast to a taut bud. Amy purred in feminine pleasure.

They touched, kissed, explored, discovered, hands and lips never still, seeking more, savoring all. Passions heightened to a fever pitch, hotter than the flames of the fire in the hearth.

"Oh, Blue, please," Amy said finally, her voice quavering.

He moved over her, catching his weight on his arms. He looked directly into her eyes, seeing what he needed to know.

He entered her slowly, so acutely aware of his size and strength, glorying in the fact that she was receiving, welcoming, all that he brought to her.

Amy's lashes drifted down as she was filled with the magnificence of Blue. He was so strong, yet tempered his power with infinite gentleness.

Blue, her mind sang. Oh, Blue. This joining, their lovemaking, was so exquisite, special, rare, so wondrous.

All rational thought fled from Amy's mind as Blue began to move within her. She matched his tempo beat for beat. The tension built, coiling within them, hotter, higher.

Then they soared beyond the storm in the heavens, bursting into a bright and spectacular place where they could only go together.

"Amy!"

"Oh, Blue."

They clung to each other, hovered there, then drifted slowly back to the soft carpeting in front of the crackling fire. Blue shifted next to Amy, encircling her waist with one arm.

"Incredible," he said, then kissed her on the temple.

"Yes," she said dreamily.

The thunder rolled in great booming waves across the heavens; lightning shattered the turbulent sky; rain poured down in torrents.

But inside the house on the Rocking B Ranch, Amy and Blue were snug and warm, sated...and together.

In front of the pretty fire in the hearth, they slept.

Amy stirred, stilled, then shifted again, finally acknowledging the unwelcomed fact that she was awake.

She'd been having a marvelous dream about swimming with Blue in a gorgeous pond edged by lush greenery. A magnificent waterfall was at one end of the pond, cascading frothy water down in a continuous roar.

Amy frowned as she opened her eyes slowly, realizing she could still hear the dim sound of the waterfall, even though she was awake. She blinked, then shot straight upward in the bed, gasping as the sheet dropped to her waist and revealed her bare breasts.

Snatching the sheet, she gripped it tightly beneath her chin with both hands as she looked frantically around the semidark room, vaguely aware that the waterfall sound was drumming rain.

Where was she? She'd never seen this room before in her life.

Her glance fell to the rumpled, empty expanse of bed next to her.

Blue, her mind whispered.

She sank back onto the pillow and drew a steadying breath. Images of what had taken place the night before in front of the fire paraded across her mind in vivid detail. A curl of heat began to pulse low in her body, and a warm flush stained her cheeks a pretty pink.

"Blue Bishop," she said aloud, rather dreamily.

Their lovemaking had been beautiful beyond belief. Magical. So very special. She had no regrets on this notorious morning after, none at all.

They were consenting adults, she reminded herself, who were free to make their own choices. They respected each other. They cared for, and about, each other.

They had also been open and honest. Blue knew she was centered on her career and was not interested in a serious relationship. No one would be hurt when she left the Rocking B at the end of her week-long assignment.

Amy reached out one hand and splayed it on Blue's pillow, gazing at the indentation where he'd laid his head.

Leave the Rocking B, her mind echoed. *Never See Blue Bishop again.* That, of course, was how it would be, *had* to be. Blue wanted a wife and children; that was very apparent from the things he had said. She

was far, far removed from entertaining the possibility
of those roles.

And so, she would leave Blue and the Rocking B
when the time came.

"Fine," she said decisively.

In the meantime, during the handful of days,
hours, left to them, she and Blue would enjoy each
other's company. They would laugh, talk, share and
make beautiful love together, because it was natural
and right.

Well, Amy decided, that covered it. All the details
had been thought through, set in order, understood.
Everything was fine and dandy.

Then why was she becoming more depressed by
the second?

"I'm not," she said aloud, throwing back the blankets on the bed. "I just need my morning coffee."

She got to her feet and looked for her clothes. Blue
had obviously carried her into his room while she
slept. Had he left her clothes scattered in front of the
fireplace?

Heavens, it was a good thing Blue didn't have a
housekeeper. The newly implemented worldliness of
Amy Madison did *not* include having strangers witnessing the evidence of her intimate business, thank
you very much.

Amy looked quickly at the clock, surprise widening her eyes when she saw that it was after 9:00 a.m.
Blue had moved quietly from the room, allowing her

to sleep late, snuggled beneath the blankets as the rain fell in a steady, soothing rhythm.

What had Blue thought, felt, she wondered, when he'd awakened and seen her sleeping next to him in his bed? What emotions were Blue dealing with in *his* morning after? Was what they had shared still falling into the arena of natural and right?

Well, there was only one way to know where she and Blue stood on this quiet, chilly, rainy morning. She had to go find him.

Amy dashed into the bathroom, wrapped a huge, fluffy towel around herself like a sarong, then hurried to her own room. As she sailed through on the way to the shower, she smiled at the neatly folded clothes that Blue had collected and placed on the bed.

A half an hour later, Amy had showered, shampooed and blow-dried her hair, then dressed in jeans and a kelly green sweater. She left the bedroom in search of Blue.

As she entered the kitchen, she heard the sound of men's laughter coming from the mud room. Opening the door, she peered into the area beyond the kitchen.

Blue and Tink were wearing wet yellow slickers, and were wrestling with something enormous that was wrapped in a brown tarp.

"Good morning," Amy said cheerfully, staying put in the doorway.

Blue looked over at her and smiled.

"There she is," he said. "Have you had breakfast?"

"No, I'm about to find some coffee. What on earth is that thing? A dead body?"

Blue chuckled. "A body probably would have been easier to maneuver. We were trying to bring this from the barn to here without getting it wet. I think we won the battle. Let's uncover it, Tink."

Amy watched intently as the tarp was carefully removed from the mysterious, lumpy bundle.

"Oh," she gasped finally, "a Christmas tree."

"Yep," Blue said, appearing extremely pleased with himself. "I've had it in the barn since last week. This is a perfect day to get it up and decorated."

"Fantastic," Amy said, smiling, her dark eyes sparkling.

"A smile before coffee?" Blue said. "This is a magical Christmas tree."

"Ms. Madison," Tink said, "I mean, Amy, I was wondering if I could take your car into the barn and putter with it today? We've done our basic chores, and the weather has us staying in. I sure would like to get my hands on that vehicle."

"Be my guest," Amy said. "I'll go get the keys for you."

When Amy came back down the hall with her key chain, she saw Blue disappearing into the room where they'd made love, the Christmas tree in tow. She gave the keys to a smiling Tink, who hustled out the door.

After pouring herself a mug of coffee, Amy started across the kitchen with the intention of joining Blue in the family room. Her step faltered, and she sank onto one of the chairs at the table. Propping her elbows on the table, she took a sip, then another, of the hot coffee.

She was, she realized, a tad nervous. She had yet to be alone with Blue since their lovemaking the night before.

Amy sighed, then continued to drink the delicious coffee.

She had so little experience in matters such as this. She *wasn't* worldly, wise and sophisticated. The nitty-gritty workings of this sort of thing were foreign to her. She didn't know how to act, what to say, when she eventually entered the room where Blue had taken the Christmas tree.

Speaking of Christmas trees, she thought with a frown, had Blue just *assumed* she was going to spend the hours necessary to decorate it with him? She *had* fully intended to work on her article, after all.

If Blue had *asked* if she would like to help trim the tree, she would have politely informed him that she simply didn't have time. Then again, maybe tree decorating was to Blue Bishop one of those male things that he preferred to do alone.

"Well," Amy said, then drained her mug, "there's only one way to find out what Blue is thinking."

She rinsed her mug, placed it in the dishwasher, then lifted her chin to what she decided was a sophisticated tilt. She marched from the kitchen.

Blue tightened the last screw on the metal stand, then stepped back to see if the Christmas tree was straight. Satisfied, he moved it into its traditional spot in front of the window.

Glancing at the doorway for the umpteenth time, he frowned.

Where was Amy? He'd figured that she would give Tink the keys to her car, grab a mug of coffee, then join him in the room where he'd carried the tree.

Should he go look for her? Ask her how long it would be before she was ready to start decorating the tree? Then it struck him. Maybe he should officially invite her to take part in trimming the tree. Hell, he just didn't know.

Blue shook his head in self-disgust at his confusion, then crossed the room. He hunkered down in front of the hearth and soon had a warming fire going. As he stood, he turned to look where he and Amy had made such incredibly beautiful love.

It had been really something, he mused. What he'd shared with Amy was beyond anything he'd known before. It was as though their bodies had truly meshed into one entity, a whole from two halves.

It went without saying that the physical release he'd experienced had been dynamite. But it was the emotions involved that had awed him, made him realize without a doubt that his joining with Amy had been rare, special, and would be reverently cherished.

He had never in his life felt so complete, so fulfilled, as he had when making love with Amy Madison. There had been a sense of having traveled so very far, searching and at last, *at long last,* found what had been missing from his life.

There had been emotions of protectiveness toward Amy, as well, along with possessiveness and the knowledge that he would stand between her and harm's way at any cost.

Blue ran one hand over the back of his neck.

Was this love? How was a guy supposed to know? How had Tux known that he was in love with his Incredibly Beautiful Nancy?

Damn, why did this love business have to be so complicated?

"Blue?"

Blue's head snapped up, and he saw Amy walking slowly into the room, stopping in the center.

His heart thundered. With her big fawn eyes, her silky curls, delicate, womanly body, there stood his Amy, and she was beautiful.

He closed the distance between them, cradled her face in his hands and looked directly into her eyes.

"Amy Madison, would you do me the honor of trimming the Christmas tree with me, here in *this* room, *our* room?"

Amy's heart melted, and her firm resolve to work on her column fled into oblivion.

"Blue," she said, matching his warm smile, "I'd be delighted to help decorate the Christmas tree."

Chapter Nine

It was fun.

At times, Amy laughed so hard at Blue's antics that her stomach hurt and her eyes filled with tears of merriment.

A Christmas tree, Blue declared at the onset, was a work of art, a creation, a happening.

According to Blue, two ornaments of the same color must *never* hang side by side, burned-out bulbs were to be replaced immediately...and tinsel? Well, tinsel was a study in perfection, he said. Each silvery strand was to be placed on the branches individually. Clumps of tinsel were definitely taboo.

Amy and Blue stood close to each other during the decorating endeavor. They would walk away to reach into the boxes Blue had brought into the room, then return to the tree, automatically moving to where the other one was.

The rain slowed to a quiet, steady fall, the fire crackled as Blue added logs as needed and time passed with smiles, laughter and a lovely sense of *I'm glad I'm here sharing this with you.*

What a glorious memory all of this will be, Amy mused at one point. She couldn't remember when the trimming of a Christmas tree had been transformed into such a special event for her. Oh, yes, she would remember this day spent with Blue. Where would she be at Christmas a year from now? At her mother's, she supposed. They would decorate the small, table-top tree, exchange gifts, have a nice meal and spend a quiet, pleasant day together.

And Blue?

Would he be married by next Christmas? Would he be decorating a tree like this one with his wife? Would this room once again ring with lovely laughter, this time shared by Mr. and Mrs. Blue Bishop?

A sudden cold knot tightened in Amy's stomach as a picture flitted in her mind of Blue reaching out toward a woman Amy couldn't see clearly in the shadowy image.

She shook her head slightly, trying to push the disturbing scenario away. She placed a strand of tinsel pencil straight on a limb of the tree, seeing with dismay that her hand was trembling.

"How are you doing, partner?" Blue said, coming

to where Amy stood. He slid one arm across her shoulders and tucked her close to his side. "Are you about ready for some lunch?"

Amy looked up at him and smiled.

The vision of Blue with that unknown woman was now completely gone, thank goodness. Blue Bishop was with Amy Madison, and that was what she would dwell on, just the moment at hand.

"I only have about a dozen or so more strands of tinsel to do," she said, "then I'll be more than ready for some food."

"Sold." The smile that had been on Blue's face changed into a serious expression. "Amy, I haven't said anything to you today about what we shared in this room last night. I don't want you to think that I took our lovemaking lightly.

"It's because it was so special that I've avoided bringing it up in fear that I wouldn't be able to find the proper words to convey how I felt. Do you understand what I'm saying?"

"Yes," Amy whispered. She blinked against sudden tears that refused to budge, tears produced by Blue's quietly spoken, heartfelt declaration of what he was feeling. "Thank you, Blue. Thank you very much. It...our lovemaking...was very special to me, too. Very, *very* special."

"Good. That's good."

Blue lowered his head and claimed her mouth in a deep kiss. When he raised his head again, he shifted

Amy around to his front, encasing her in the protective cocoon of his strong arms.

Amy's hands floated upward to encircle Blue's neck, and their lips met once more. The tinsel in Amy's fingers fell to the floor in a glittering, silvery cascade.

Blue's hands slid over the slope of Amy's buttocks, nestling her to the cradle of his hips, his arousal full and heavy against her.

"I want you," he said, close to her lips.

"Yes, but..."

"Hmm?" he said, trailing a ribbon of kisses along her slender throat.

"Your men," she said breathlessly. "What if—?"

"The rule is," Blue interrupted, "if the door to the mud room is locked, I don't want company, unless it's an extreme emergency. That door is definitely locked."

"Oh."

"Amy, do you have any idea what you're doing to me? You're turning me inside out...not just my body, but my head, my mind. I've never felt so... Hell, I don't know what this is."

"Does it have to have a name? It's special, Blue, we know that. It's ours to share. I'm here. You're here. What matters is the moment we're living in. I want you, Blue Bishop. I truly do."

"The moment we're living in?" Blue repeated. "What about tomorrow, the future, the—?"

Amy stilled his words by rising to her toes and brushing her lips over his.

"But—"

"Blue Bishop, you are a fussbudget today," Amy said, smiling. "I thought I was bad worrying about details and having everything organized. The only thing you have to concern yourself about right now is whether you want to make love with me before, or after, lunch."

Blue laughed and swung her up into his arms.

"Both," he said, holding her tightly to his chest. "We'll make love, have lunch, make love, make love, make love…"

Their mingled, joyous laughter danced through the air as Blue carried Amy from the room.

Two in the morning.

Blue stifled a groan of frustration as he looked yet again at the clock on the nightstand next to the bed.

Dawn and the need to get up would be here in a handful of hours, and he hadn't slept a wink. Every muscle in his body ached from lying as still as possible, instead of tossing, turning and punching his pillow, so as not to disturb Amy, who slumbered peacefully beside him.

Blue's eyes had long since grown accustomed to the darkness, and he could clearly see Amy, her head nestled on his pillow. He shifted slightly to enable him to sift his fingers through her silky dark curls, a smile touching his lips.

In the next instant, he frowned, dropped his hand heavily onto the bed and stared up at the ceiling.

On the surface, he knew, the day would qualify for as close to perfection as was possible. He and Amy had shut out the world and concentrated solely on each other. They'd laughed, talked, shared, made glorious love over and over, tucked away memories that were special and important.

They'd exchanged stories of their childhoods, their mischievous antics, their adolescent rebellions and heartbreaks, their trepidation at leaving home for college to meet the challenges of the beckoning world beyond the safe haven of their loving families.

They'd learned more about each other, understood and respected more. They'd made love so exquisitely it was as though a magical force had created them, one for the other, the missing half of whom they needed in order to be a whole.

Ah, yes, it was all so perfect.

But, no, it wasn't.

Blue sighed, then carefully slipped from the bed, easing away from Amy's warm, naked body that fit so symmetrically along his.

He strode to the window and brushed back the drapes enough to see that a light rain continued to fall, although the thunder and lightning had moved on to other parts of the heavens.

Blue sighed.

He wished that he could just savor the hours spent with Amy and quit analyzing everything to death.

But that would mean running from what was causing him to lose sleep and becoming painfully aware of a tight, cold knot in his gut.

Blue Bishop didn't run from anything, never had, never would. He was one of the Bishop boys, and they squared off against anything that stood in their path.

Amy Madison.

So many times during the lovely day they'd spent together, he'd attempted to broach the subject of the future. Each time, Amy delivered her pat little speech of living only for the moment.

Hell, Blue thought, shaking his head, he couldn't get Amy to make a commitment about whether she would be willing to try some of his secret-recipe pancakes for breakfast tomorrow morning, instead of just having her usual coffee-only meal.

He'd been dismally aware by late evening that if he spoke of next week, or next month, Amy immediately launched into a dissertation regarding her career: who might be an interesting subject for her A Week In The Life Of... column, her need to produce the stories faster, her desire to have a printer at home so she could work more efficiently when away from the office.

Amy made it clear, over and over, that her career came first. No, it was worse than that. Her career was the be-all and end-all of her existence, her focus, her reason for being.

Blue yanked the drapes closed with more force than was necessary.

Damn it, he didn't care how many times, or in how many ways, Amy drove home her message, hitting him right in his heart, his very soul.

He didn't believe her.

Oh, yeah, he believed that she believed what she was saying was the truth. But he did *not* believe that what she believed should be believed.

Oh, Lord, *he* was babbling like an idiot.

Blue dragged both hands down his face, then drew a steadying breath.

He'd known more than one career woman in his singles'-scene days. He'd been happy to hook up with them for a while, because they wanted nothing from him but to be wined, dined, then engage in healthy, no-strings sex.

They were dynamic, forceful women who considered themselves equal to, or better than, men, and had submerged the softer side of their femininity beneath a rather brittle exterior.

In bed, they were energetic partners, giving of their bodies willingly. But it was more a series of exercises, without any emotions involved.

And, by damn, he didn't care how many times Amy Madison declared herself to be a true-blue career-only woman, *she didn't fit the mold.*

Amy's femininity, her womanliness, was a nearly tangible aura surrounding her. Her big, dark fawn eyes displayed her feelings; they actually sparkled when she laughed, grew misty when she spoke of missing her father, had a little-girl honesty and innocence when relating tales of her youth, were smoky with desire when she reached for him.

She wasn't brittle; she was soft, and not just her beautiful, slender body, but her outlooks and attitudes, as well.

Amy didn't engage in casual sex; she made love, giving not only of her body, but holding back nothing of her caring for him, her emotions. He'd felt it. She'd come to him totally, keeping nothing hidden or protected.

Amy Madison could, if she allowed herself, fall in love with a man with an intensity that defied description. She could, if she allowed herself, nurture a child born of the union with that man and love that baby beyond measure.

Amy was a woman first, a career person second.

Yes, Blue thought, it was true. Damn it, it was true.

And somehow he had to show Amy that truth.

Why did it matter so much to him? Why was he now pacing the floor of his bedroom in the middle of the night, instead of getting the sleep he so desperately needed?

He'd asked himself the complicated question of whether or not he'd fallen head over heels in love with Amy Madison, but he sure as hell hadn't gotten a clear-cut answer.

All he was certain of was that his feelings for Amy

and the emotional intensity of their lovemaking had never happened to him before.

He had to know what it all meant.

He had to!

If this was indeed love, then he was going to fight to keep it, to keep Amy in his life, as his wife, forever. In order to do that, he had to be patient yet persistent in his quest to get Amy to recognize, accept and embrace, who she really was.

But what if he accomplished that goal, only to have Amy discover that while she cared for Blue, she certainly wasn't in love with him. What if she took her newly found self and marched right into the arms of another man?

"Damn," Blue said, dragging both hands roughly through his hair. "Stop thinking, Bishop."

Amy stirred on the bed, and Blue stood statue still, hardly breathing, hoping he hadn't wakened her with his outburst. She settled again, and he crept back to the bed, feeling like a naked thief in the night in his own house.

He slid into bed, carefully, slowly, then curved like a spoon next to Amy's delicate body.

"Mmm," he murmured, savoring the feel of her soft, warm skin.

He wrapped one arm around her waist, closed his eyes and, mercifully, slept.

Amy sat at the kitchen table and sipped her coffee as Blue shrugged into the yellow slicker. A misty, chilly rain continued to fall.

"This day in the life of a rancher," he said, snapping the slicker, "is pure drudgery, with wet and cold thrown in for good measure. After a high-wind rainstorm like we had, we check fences. Exciting, huh?"

"Well, I'll put it in my report," Amy said, smiling, "and at least make it sound extremely important."

Blue nodded. "It is. Downed fences mean cattle wandering where they aren't supposed to be."

"Got it."

Blue moved to her side, set her mug on the table, then took both of her hands and urged her to her feet. Amy went willingly.

Blue lowered his head and kissed her so intensely that she swayed when he released her, then ended up plopping back down on her chair.

"Goodness," she said, splaying one hand on her racing heart.

Blue chuckled. "Hold that thought. I'll see you later. I'm glad you listened to reason and agreed you didn't need to be out there with me in this messy weather to make your column authentic."

Amy shrugged. "I'm a reasonable person...most of the time."

Blue's smile disappeared.

"Are you?" he said quietly. "Are you open to new ways of looking at things?"

Amy cocked her head slightly to one side, confusion evident on her face.

"I like to think so," she said. "I know I'm missing the point here, Blue. What is it you're trying to say?"

Blue looked at her for a long moment, then shook his head.

"I've got to go." He dropped a quick kiss on her lips. "Have a nice day. Treat this place as though it was your own. Just do whatever you want to. See ya."

He turned and strode out of the kitchen through the door leading to the mud room.

"See ya," Amy said softly to the empty room.

She picked up the mug and sipped the brew, allowing the silence, broken only by the steady fall of the rain, to settle in around her.

Treat this place as though it was your own.

Blue's words echoed in Amy's mind. She swept her gaze over the large kitchen, unable to curb her imagination. She propped one elbow on the table and rested her chin in her hand.

She wouldn't change this room, she decided, if it was hers to do so. It was bright on a sunny day, cheerful and welcoming.

She would, however, add a perky set of canisters to line up along the back of one of the counters. Blue kept sugar and flour in coffee cans in the cupboards. Yes, canisters...maybe with sunflowers on them, or violets, or...

"Cows," she said, with a bubble of laughter.

* * *

Hours later, Amy sat on the sofa in front of the fire she'd managed to produce in the hearth. She'd turned on the lights on the Christmas tree and settled in to work on her column. With a feeling of satisfaction, she pressed several buttons on the small keyboard of her computer, turned it off and set it on the floor.

She stretched leisurely, raising her arms above her head, then dropping them into her lap.

The story was coming together beautifully, she mused. She wouldn't have believed she could make order out of the chaos of her notes until the assignment week was completed, but she had.

The first half of the column was finished. She had an additional set of paragraphs fine-tuned and ready to be slipped into place when she finally decided where they should best go.

Gibson McKinley had been right. She *was* capable of doing two of her features a month. She'd been too self-indulgent with her demand for time to do extensive research before beginning a new week in the life of whomever.

What had Blue asked her that morning? Oh, yes, was she open to new ways of looking at things? Well, she obviously was, as evidenced by the approach she was now taking to writing her column.

But what had *Blue* meant by his question? What had he been referring to with such a serious expression on his face and tone to his voice? She really didn't know.

With a shrug of confusion, Amy got to her feet and headed for the kitchen with the intention of deciding what to prepare for dinner.

The meal of hamburgers, French fries, tossed salad and more of the weird-looking chocolate cake with *lots* of maple frosting was probably tasty, Blue thought hazily as he ate. But he was so beat he hardly knew his name, let alone whether or not he was enjoying his dinner.

The combination of lack of sleep from the previous night and a long, grueling day in the saddle had wiped him out. He was accustomed to feeling this way on occasion, as there were days on the Rocking B that pushed a man's body to its limit and beyond. He didn't mind when it happened; he simply crashed into bed for hours of recuperating sleep.

But what was Amy thinking while he sat there like a sludge, hardly capable of contributing to dinnertime conversation? She'd been alone in the house all day, and was now sitting across the table from a zombie, who was going to have to head for bed as soon as he ate the maple frosting that had a dab of cake attached to it.

This was *not* good, not good at all. Hearth and home would tally up to boring as hell to Amy at the rate he was going.

"Blue?"

"Hmm?"

"Oh, Blue, you're exhausted," Amy said, smiling at him gently. "I don't want to sound like a nag telling you what to do, but may I suggest that you go to bed as soon as you're finished eating?"

Blue blinked. "What?"

"I said, why don't you—?"

"Yes, I heard you," he interrupted, "and that's exactly what I need to do. But what about you, Amy? I left you alone all day, and I'm about to desert you for the entire evening."

"Heavens, I don't need to be entertained. I'm perfectly capable of filling my leisure hours on my own." She flapped her hands at him. "Shoo. Go to bed, go to sleep. If you land facedown in the cake, I'm afraid the frosting might adhere itself to you for life. Good night, Blue Bishop."

Blue planted his hands flat on the table and pushed himself to his feet, his eyes riveted on Amy. He came around the table and drew her up into his embrace.

"Thank you for being so understanding," he said. "It means a lot, it really does. You're a very special lady, Amy."

"Well, thank you, sir."

"Listen, before I forget. Tomorrow night I'm supposed to be at my folks' for dinner. I'll call my mom in the morning and ask her to set a place for you at the table."

"Oh, but—"

"Shh. I don't have the energy to debate the issue.

This week in the life of a Texas rancher happens to include dinner with his family. You can meet my twin brother, Bram, Tux and his wife, Nancy, and my parents. Okay?''

"It sounds delightful, and I accept your gracious invitation."

"Good." He paused. "Amy, please come into my bed later. I want to wake up next to you in the morning." He brushed his lips over hers, causing her to shiver from the feathery caress. "Yes?"

"Yes," she whispered.

"Good," he said, then claimed her mouth in a searing, toe-curling kiss.

When Blue finally released Amy, she could hardly breathe, and heated desire was thrumming throughout her. Blue mumbled good-night and shuffled from the room. Amy could do nothing more than waggle her fingers in farewell, then sink onto her chair.

"Even dead tired, the man is potent stuff," she finally managed to say to the empty room.

Let's see, she thought, pressing one fingertip to her chin. She would clean up the kitchen, put more logs on the fire in the hearth of her favorite room, which included the Christmas tree, then find a novel to read from the selection on the bookshelves.

Humming softly, she began to clear the table, only to stop halfway across the room and frown.

Was she acting like a little girl playing house? she wondered. She was thoroughly enjoying planning and preparing meals, mentally adding canisters to the kitchen counter, sitting by a fire in the colorful glow of the Christmas tree. Why was she having such fun and registering such a sense of fulfillment?

Amy shook her head. She didn't need to add any more confusing questions to the unanswered stack already in her befuddled mind. And besides, when she slipped into bed next to Blue later that night, there would be nothing *little girl* about the *woman* who would nestle herself along Blue Bishop's magnificent naked body.

Resuming her humming, Amy continued with the task of cleaning the kitchen to sparkling perfection.

Chapter Ten

Blue pressed on the brake of the shiny pickup truck and folded his arms on top of the steering wheel, allowing the vehicle to idle.

"Well," he said, looking out the side window, "there goes a piece of history. They're tearing down the house on the Bar None. That place was built somewhere around the turn of the century."

Amy leaned forward to see past Blue.

"That's sad," she said.

"That's progress." Blue straightened and started driving again. "They're going to transform the place into a dude-ranch deal, according to Chaps." He chuckled. "For a guy that rarely leaves the spread, Chaps sure knows what's going on in these parts at any given moment."

"They should have restored the house," Amy
said, frowning. "Fixed it up and kept it standing.
They could have offered a stay in an authentic historical home as part of their vacation package. I think
that destroying that home is simply awful."

Blue smacked the steering wheel with the palm of
one hand.

"Well, that settles it," he said. "I'll go over to
the Bar None tomorrow with my shotgun and tell
those yahoos to quit pulling that old place down. *And*
to put back everything they've torn off. How's
that?"

"Thank you. That will do nicely," Amy said, with
a burst of laughter. She sobered in the next instant.
"Seriously, though, Blue, imagine the stories that
house could tell if walls could talk. Generations of
the same family may have lived there, one after the
next."

"They did. It belonged to the same clan all these
years. It was sold for back taxes when the old man
died. His son didn't want any part of ranching. I
bought that piano at the estate sale, remember? Tux's
wife got an ancient jar of buttons. Man, she was so
excited. She owns a shop called Buttons and Beads,
so that dusty bottle was a real treasure to her."

"See? She appreciates history. Darn it, they
should have preserved that house."

"Amy, Amy, Amy," Blue said, shaking his head,
"I thought you were open to new ideas."

"I am but... Never mind. I won't get on another rip about it."

"So you still think you have an open mind about new ways of looking at things?"

"Yes, of course."

"That's good." Blue paused. "Say, when we get home tonight, how about playing some Christmas carols on the piano? Do you know any?"

"A few, but I'm not a very accomplished piano player. My poor mother tried so hard to teach me, but I just couldn't master it. My mother plays so beautifully. She was with a small symphony when she met and married my father. She was well on her way to a brilliant career."

"And?"

"She gave it up to be a wife and mother. A career like that would have required a great deal of travel, and she felt it wasn't conducive to having the family life she wanted for my father and me. She had to pick between her career and her family."

He now had the answer to the mystifying question of why Amy felt a woman couldn't have both a career and a family, Blue thought.

"I take it your mother is a tad bitter about where she could have gone with her music, but didn't."

"Heavens, no. Why would you think that?"

"Well, you have very strong feelings about choosing between career or marriage. I'm assuming your mother taught you that early on."

"Not really. When I asked her how she'd met my

father, she told me he'd attended a performance of the symphony, then came backstage afterward and the rest is history. Anyway, my mother has always seemed very satisfied with her life.

"*I* realized, though, what she'd sacrificed for me and my father. I drew my own conclusions regarding the fact that a woman must choose her path and stay focused on it."

"Amy, come on. There are a multitude of women who combine family and career."

"Yes, and there are a multitude of articles appearing one after the other about how exhausted those women are, how frustrated and unhappy, because there's never enough time, not enough of her to go around. She feels as though every arena of her life gets shortchanged. And forget about a niche for herself. Or private time. It rarely happens."

"It wouldn't have to be that way for you."

"Why would I be any different from the rest? Facts are facts, Blue."

"Oh? Think about this. You're working on a column for the *Holler*, giving it your maximum effort. Yet you have still prepared dinner every night you've been at the Rocking B. You even had time to do a family-type thing like trimming the Christmas tree."

"Yes, well...well, what if my assignment would have been in town? I'd have been tearing in the door, throwing fast food on the table and spending the evening organizing my notes from that day. Where do you see time for a husband and children in *that* scenario?''

Blue glared at her, then redirected his attention to the road.

''You're not giving the husband any credit at all,'' he said. ''He helps make dinner. He helps with the kids, the housework, the errands. Together, they make it work. Together, Amy.''

She shook her head. ''But I wouldn't be the best I could be at any of those roles. That's very important to me, Blue. I'm not prepared to make the kind of sacrifices that my mother did.''

''Your mother is happy!''

''Don't yell at me!''

''Sorry,'' he mumbled.

''Could we change the subject? We're heading for a quarrel, and there's no point in that.''

''Yeah, okay,'' Blue said, sighing, ''but you're stubborn as a rock, and you're *not* open to new ideas.''

''*This* topic is what you were referring to when you asked me if I was?''

''Yes!''

''Well, then you're right. I'm *not* open to reviewing my stand on the issue. I can't. I know who I am, where I'm going and what it will take to get there.''

''Is that a fact? I recall that you had your heart set on writing children's books, but you discovered it wasn't a viable choice. So you changed, adjusted, went in another direction. Right?''

"Yes, but—"

"Hear me out. You gathered new data and kept an open mind about the best direction to go. Hell, a person would never know you were capable of being that flexible.

"Amy, I believe that a person should go after what they want, be willing to work hard, earn it. That's what my parents taught their sons. Damn it, Amy, if you really wanted a career *and* a family, you'd find a way to do it. Your negative attitude is getting very old, very quickly."

"Well, excuse me to hell and back, Mr. Bishop."

"No, I won't excuse you," he said, none too quietly. "You're copping out. Why don't you just admit you don't want to be a wife and mother? Quit harping on this you-can't-have-both crap. If you really wanted both, you'd find a way to do it.

"You, Amy Madison, don't want anything to do with looking across the breakfast table at the same man every morning for the rest of your life. And diapers? Formula? PTA? Chicken pox? Not on your life. Why don't you just knock off the make-your-choice bit and be honest with yourself?"

Bishop, Blue thought, *you are a dead man.* He'd pushed Amy right to the wall. A quick glance in her direction showed him fury in its purest form. Oh, yeah, Amy was mad as hell.

He'd used reverse psychology. Now Amy was supposed to holler her head off and say he was all wrong, that she *did* want to have a husband and children, and find a way to combine those roles with her career.

But Amy wasn't speaking up.

Damn, she didn't even look angry anymore. She had a rather perplexed expression on her face and was staring off into space. What was going on in that complicated female mind of hers? Had he totally blown it? Or had what he'd done been brilliant?

Why wasn't Amy saying anything?

"Why aren't you saying anything, Amy?" he said.

"I'm thinking."

"Could you think a little faster, then make a comment or two?"

"I don't know, Blue. That was a lot that you threw at me. I've always prided myself on being in touch with the inner me, but what if you're right?"

No! Blue's mind hammered. What had he done? His reverse psychology had backfired big time. Amy was actually examining the possibility that what he'd yelled about might be true, might be how she really felt. Damn it!

"Look," he said, "I shouldn't have said all that. It's a worthless theory."

"Maybe it's not. This is so grim. I feel like a stranger in my own body, needing to discover who I really am." Amy sighed. "Blue Bishop, since I met you, I've been more confused about more things than I have in my entire life."

A flicker of hope tapped against Blue's heart. "That's good."

"Thanks a lot," Amy said dryly.

"What I mean is, confusion indicates that serious thought is necessary regarding topics you figured were done deals. You've now got to take a fresh look with an open mind. Right?"

Amy frowned. "I guess so."

"I know so."

Amy nodded slowly as Blue pulled into the driveway at his parents' house.

The Bishop family was delightful, Amy thought. Blue's brothers, sister-in-law and his parents, Jana-John and Abe, were all open, warm and friendly.

Despite the rather absentminded aura emanating from Abe, he managed to convey his love for his wife, sons and daughter-in-law.

Jana-John was...well, *enchanting* was a perfect word to describe her. She reminded Amy of an angel who should be set carefully in the specially reserved place on top of a Christmas tree.

Tux and Bram had the same sapphire-colored eyes as Blue. The brothers looked alike, with similar muscled physiques on tall frames, but they remained uniquely individual. Their hair was the biggest contrast: Tux's was very blond, Bram's brown with sun streaks of near-blond and Blue's was as dark as a raven's wing.

Oh, yes, Amy mused, they were dynamic, handsome and masculinity personified, these Bishop brothers.

Nancy, Tux's wife, was vivacious and fun. She had gorgeous dark hair, wild and tumbled, like a gypsy's, and it suited her perfectly. She'd chattered away, telling Amy about the new location of her store, Buttons and Beads, as though the two of them had been friends for years.

This house, Amy thought, glancing around the living room, despite its mix-match of furniture and rather weird striped carpeting, overflowed with love. She could feel it, as though it were nearly a tangible presence. It was like an invisible blanket a person could wrap around herself and snuggle in.

Was it possible, as Blue had proposed, that she really didn't want this type of hearth, home and happiness in her life?

"You all must be hungry," Jana-John said. "I'll get dinner on the table."

"I'll help," Nancy said, getting to her feet.

"So will I," Amy said.

"Amy, dear," Jana-John said as the women left the room, "what do you think of the Rocking B?"

"I'm going to wash up," Abe said, wandering away.

The minute that Abe disappeared from view, Bram and Tux strode across the living room and settled on the sofa, sandwiching Blue between them.

"Report, Blue," Bram said, keeping his voice low. "Your Amy is pretty as a picture. She's got a good sense of humor, is friendly, easy to talk to, the whole enchilada. You have a bona fide wife candidate there, that's for sure. How's it going?''

Blue sighed and shook his head.

''Thank you for sharing,'' Tux said dryly. ''Come on, Blue, spill it.''

''Tux,'' Blue said, ''how did you know you were in love with Nancy? I mean, how did you really, honest-to-goodness *know* you wanted to marry her and spend the rest of your life with her, until death do you part?''

''Oh,'' Tux said. ''Well, let's see. Do you think about Amy when you're apart? Count the minutes until you'll be together again? Can you see her so clearly in your mind's eye at any given moment that you'd swear you could reach out and touch, hold, kiss her?

''Would you lay your life on the line for her? When you make love...forget that. We'll skip the personal stuff.''

''That's a lot of questions to dump on a guy all at once, Tux,'' Bram said. ''Back up and give them to Blue one at a time.''

''Yes,'' Blue said.

''Yes...what?'' Bram asked.

''To all those questions, my answer is yes.''

Tux whopped Blue on the knee. ''Hot damn, you're in love, little brother.''

''I am? Why do *you* know that and *I* don't?''

''Because you've never been in love before,'' Tux said. ''You're speaking to a man of experience here.

I know love when I see it in front of my nose now, because I'm in love with my Nancy. Get it?''

"Makes sense," Bram said. "Man, oh man, Blue is in love. Now I'm really the odd man out."

"Can it, Bram," Tux said. "Your day will come. Now then, Blue, how does Amy feel about you?"

Blue frowned. "She cares." He looked at Tux, then Bram, who were staring at him. "What?"

"That's it?" Tux said. "She cares?"

Blue dragged both hands down his face. "It's so damn complicated. I've blown this so badly it's a crime.

"Amy believes she can't have a family and a career, because she wouldn't be top-of-the-line in all the different roles that encompasses. I believe *she* believes that, but I do *not* believe it's true. She *is* capable of having it all, because there's so much to her, so much love to give.

"But I used reverse psychology on her, insisting that she was using her career as an excuse to keep from admitting that she didn't really want a husband and kids."

"Lord, you're stupid," Bram said.

"No joke," Blue said miserably. "I thought I'd trigger a response from her that she *could* have a family and her work if she set her mind to it. But, now she says I might just have a valid point there, and she'd better examine the real inner her, or some such thing."

"Really dumb," Bram reiterated.

"Shut up, Bram," Blue said. "I don't see you bouncing your babies on your knee. *Your* wife isn't in the kitchen helping serve up the heaven-only-knows-what-it-is our mother made for dinner."

"*My* wife is in the kitchen," Tux said, "so I have credentials. That was a really dumb thing to do, Blue."

"Amen," Bram said.

Blue lunged to his feet. "So now what? I'm in a helluva mess here. That woman is driving me crazy."

"Yep," Tux said, "that's love."

"Love," Blue said, suddenly smiling. "Yeah. I *am* in love with Amy Madison. Isn't that something? Isn't that great?" He shook his head and frowned. "No, it's not, because I stand a very good chance of having her walk out of my life when her assignment at the ranch for the *Holler* is completed. What in the hell am I going to do?"

"Hey, I know what you're going through," Tux said. "Remember when I thought I'd lost Nancy to...well, to herself, to what she believed to be true? She was convinced that loving someone meant you were turning over the control of your life to that person and losing a part of yourself."

"Yeah, you were in a bad way back then," Bram said. "You upset our mother, because she realized you were really down. Blue and I had to pay you a visit because you had our mother in a dither, and that's against the rules of the Bishop family."

"Those were the darkest days of my life," Tux said, shaking his head.

"Can we quit skipping down memory lane?" Blue said. "*My* future happiness is at stake now."

"Right," Tux said. "Well, I left Nancy alone during my bad patch. Actually, to be honest, I'd given up, couldn't think of one more thing to say that might change her mind about how she viewed marriage. She worked it through on her own and came to me." Tux glanced heavenward. "Thank you, thank you, thank you."

"Amy still has some days left at the ranch to finish her assignment," Blue said. "I've got to put that time to good use."

"Oh, you're doing dandy so far," Bram said, then snorted in disgust. "You had enough to deal with regarding Amy's theory that she can't have marriage and a career. Then you added to the mix that she might not even *want* to be a wife and mother, you dolt."

"I know, I know." Blue threw out his arms. "So what do I do?"

"Don't push her," Tux said. "Stay very alert, listen to everything she says. For each negative statement she makes, come back with a positive one." He paused and ran one hand over his chin. "For example, if Amy says her career is fantastic, you say that's fine, but will her career keep her warm on a winter night? Get it? It's brilliant."

"Corny," Bram said.

"I'm desperate," Blue interjected. "I'll try anything."

Tux got to his feet and placed one hand on Blue's shoulder.

"Hang in there, little brother," Tux said. "Listen to me, though. These are the words of a veteran of the battle. Women are wonderful. However, women are a tad weird. Just when you think you're beginning to understand what makes your lady tick... wham...off she goes in another direction."

"Keep it up, Tux," Blue said, glaring at him. "I was already depressed, remember?"

"My point is," Tux went on, "you have to stay on your toes. And, Blue? Don't give up. I did. I thought I'd lost Nancy forever. Thank God she came around on her own. Don't run that risk. Stick like glue to Amy, but do it with finesse. Don't think that hollering your head off will get you anywhere."

"Excuse me," Bram said. "I realize I have none of the credentials you do, Tux, but I think there's a major piece missing from your pearly words of wisdom."

"Which is?" Tux said.

"Blue should wait for the right moment, the proper setting," Bram said, "and tell Amy Madison that he is in love with her and is humbly asking her to be his wife."

"Oh, Lord," Blue whispered.

"You gotta do it, Blue," Bram insisted.

"Good point," Tux said. "Not bad, Bram. There's

hope for you, there really is. All you need to do is find the right woman to work your mighty mind on."

"Yeah, right," Bram said. "They all left town. Hell, they all left the state of Texas."

"Ask Amy to marry me?" Blue said, staring into space. "She'll say no. Guaranteed."

"At first, yes, I imagine she will," Tux said, "but you can bet she'll be thinking about your proposal, along with the other stuff in her head. Women are so-o-o strange."

"Why can't they be easy to understand, uncomplicated like we men are?" Blue asked.

"Beats me," Tux said, shrugging. "Sure would make life simpler if women were as clear-cut as men. You know, what you see is what you get. But then again, maybe life wouldn't be as interesting that way."

"I love you, Amy," Blue said. "Will you marry me? Will you marry me, Amy? I love you. Oh, hell, I'm a wreck, a basket case."

Bram got up and patted Blue on the back.

"I'm putting my money on you, Blue," Bram said. "My dime says there will be another Bishop brother wedding in the near future."

"I hope so," Blue said. "Man, oh man, I really hope so."

"I just wish," Bram said, sounding totally miserable, "that the wedding was going to be mine."

Chapter Eleven

The night was chilly, but clear, as Amy and Blue drove back to the Rocking B. Stars were blinking in the velvety, dark sky as though a switch had been thrown to produce a beautiful, synchronized display of glittering diamonds.

Amy was quiet, and Blue kept sliding quick, anxious glances in her direction while maneuvering through the heavy Houston traffic. When they at last left the city with its congestion and noise, the silence in the cab of the truck pushed his nerves to the edge.

"So!" he said much too loudly.

Amy jerked in her seat at his sudden outburst.

"That was quite a dinner my mother prepared, wasn't it?" Blue said, striving for a lighthearted tone of voice. He chuckled. "She's really something, my mother."

Amy smiled. "Your mother is delightful. As for dinner...well, I can now say I've had a Christmasy meal comprised entirely of red and green food."

"Yep. Red Jell-O, green Jell-O. Red and green apple slices. Ham with red cranberry sauce. Mashed potatoes colored green. Green beans. Oh, and doughnuts with red frosting for dessert."

"Indeed. Well, she explained that since Nancy and Tux were inviting everyone to their new home on Christmas Day for dinner, she wanted to add her festive touch while you were gathered around this evening. I thought it was charming. I liked your family very much, Blue."

"They're special people." He paused. "Listen, thanks for gushing over my mother's paintings she showed you. We all know she's a terrible painter, but we wouldn't hurt her feelings for the world. We just don't ever get around to hanging any of those disasters on our walls. I don't think she has ever figured that out."

"She obviously enjoys painting," Amy said. "That's what counts. She's doing what gives her a great deal of pleasure."

Blue nodded. "Exactly."

"Jana-John Bishop is very fortunate." Amy sighed. "I envy her because she knows who she is and what she needs to do to feel fulfilled."

"Ah, Amy," Blue said, "you sound so sad. Can't

you just forget what I said about your not really wanting a husband and children? I was way out of line, and I apologize. Erase it from your mind. Please?''

''I can't, Blue. So much has happened so quickly since I met you. I'm a muddled mess, I really am. I just need some time to sort through this jumble in my mind.''

Now was the time he should add that he loved her and wanted to marry her, Blue thought frantically. But he didn't want to propose to Amy while driving along a dusty road in a pickup truck!

''Hold that thought for when we get home,'' he said. ''Okay?''

Amy pressed her fingertips to her temples.

''I wish you'd stop that,'' she said crossly.

''Stop what? What did I do?''

''Twice now you've said 'when we get home.' You did it on the way into town, and you just used the phrase again. *We* aren't going to get home. *You're* going home. I'm just a guest who's tagging along.''

''Semantics, my dear,'' Blue said, smiling. ''Hold that thought, too. Let's change the subject.''

Amy folded her arms over her breasts.

''Whatever,'' she said, definitely sounding grumpy.

''When we were having dinner,'' Blue said, deciding not to address Amy's rapidly deteriorating mood, ''my mother asked me if all my guys at the ranch had somewhere to go for Christmas. She worries about that every year.''

Amy nodded.

''I assured her that the folks at the Double W were having their annual get-together for the cowboys in the area without families. Tink and Ricky are going home. Chaps and Joe will go over to the Double W.''

''Yes, I remember you saying all that.''

''Then my mother asked you what *you* do on Christmas, but then Tux got a beep on his beeper and things got a bit hectic for a moment. You never answered my mother's question.''

Silence.

''Hello? Amy? Are you with me here? What do you do on Christmas Day?''

''I...I usually go to my mother's house.''

''Usually? As in, this year you're not?''

Silence.

''Is this a difficult question for some reason?'' Blue asked.

Amy sighed. ''No, of course not. My aunt and uncle, who live in Florida, decided to go on a holiday cruise and invited my mother and me to join them.''

''And?''

''Well, I can't take off that long from work. They'll be gone from the day before Christmas Eve until after the New Year. It took weeks for me to convince my mother to go and to assure her that I'd be just fine here. She finally agreed to it...very reluctantly...but I'm sure she'll have a marvelous time.''

"You're going to be alone on Christmas?"

Amy shrugged. "My mother and I will have a nice dinner and exchange gifts early. That will be my Christmas and, no, I won't be alone, if you look at it that way.''

"Amy, that's no good. That's bad. Awful. No way. Nope. You can come to Nancy and Tux's with me. It's settled, all right?"

"I—"

"Don't answer. Just hold that thought."

Amy laughed. "You've got me holding so many thoughts, I'm running out of holding room.''

"Sit tight. We're almost home. I mean, *I'm* almost home and... Oh, hell, forget it. The good ol' Rocking B is just up ahead.''

At the ranch, they entered the house and Blue grabbed Amy's hand. He led her into the room with the Christmas tree, turned on the tree lights, then pointed to the sofa. Amy plunked down with a sigh.

After starting a fire in the hearth, Blue turned to look at Amy, shoving both hands into the back pockets of his jeans.

She was so beautiful, he thought. In the glow of the fire and the multicolored lights on the tree, his Amy was absolutely beautiful.

And he loved her.

With every breath in his body, he was deeply and

irrevocably in love with the delicate, complicated, lovely woman sitting before him.

Oh, yes, they were home. They had driven home from the city. To their home. Together. Blue Bishop and the future Mrs. Amy Madison Bishop were home.

It sounded so good, so right.

"Amy..."

"Blue..."

They spoke at the same time, then stopped, smiling slightly.

"You first, ma'am," Blue said with a quick nod.

Amy folded her hands in her lap, stared at them for a long moment, then drew a steadying breath as she lifted her head slowly to meet Blue's gaze.

"I...I...Blue, I'm leaving the Rocking B tomorrow," she said, her voice trembling.

Of all the things that Amy might have said, her announcement was the last thing Blue had expected to hear.

He felt as though he'd been kicked in the gut by a very big and very powerful bull. A chill swept through him, despite the fact that he was standing in front of the roaring fire in the hearth.

He started to speak, realized he had no air in his lungs and took a rough breath. Pulling his hands free from his pockets, he moved to the sofa, sitting down next to Amy at an angle so he could look directly at her.

"I don't understand," he said. "Amy, what's going on here?"

She shifted her position toward him, but stared at her hands. Blue placed one long finger beneath her chin and raised her head gently.

"Amy?"

"I gave this serious thought as we were driving home...driving back to the ranch," she said softly. "I have all the material I need for my column. This isn't the busiest time of year on the Rocking B, and Chaps filled me in on branding, selling the cattle at the best time and the season when calves are born."

"But—"

"Hush, please, Blue, let me finish." Unexpected and definitely unwelcome tears misted Amy's eyes. She blinked them away. "It's not just because I finished ahead of schedule."

She took a shuddering breath.

"I *need* to leave, Blue. I have to be alone. I need time to think, to sift and sort through the maze in my mind. I'm so confused, so terribly muddled up.

"I'm not the same person I was when I arrived here. I'm not. It's hard to believe it has only been a handful of days since I came, when I realize how different I am from the Amy Madison who drove my rickety car to your front walk in a billow of dust."

"Amy, listen to me. I—"

"Wait," she said, tears echoing in her voice. "You've become so important to me, Blue, you really have. I don't even know who 'me' is anymore.

Before I came here I knew, *I knew*. Now I just don't.''

Blue covered both of Amy's hands with his.

''Amy, please forget what I said about your not wanting a husband and children. Don't think about that nonsense.''

''I have to, don't you see? And there's so much more, too. I was so cocky, so certain I could have a worldly, sophisticated fling, go to bed with you, make love, then just walk away with a flip of my hand and a casual farewell.''

''Are you sorry we made love? Do you regret it now?''

''Oh, no, Blue, no, because it was so beautiful. No, my mistake was in believing I could just wrap it up and tuck it away in a special place, then forget it happened. I could take out the memories, cherish them when I wanted to, I thought, and go about my business as before.''

''But?''

''It's all mixed-up, Blue. I'm questioning every-thing...*everything*. My career, my future, my feel-ings for you, my inner needs, who I am. I have to go. I have to be left alone to think. Please, Blue, don't make this any more difficult for me than it is. Ask Tink to bring my car out of the barn so I can leave first thing in the morning.''

Blue got to his feet and went to the hearth. He braced his hands on the mantel and stared at the leap-ing, crackling flames.

Amy looked at him, tears closing her throat. She drank in the sight of his tall, muscular body, the width of his shoulders, his powerful legs.

She wanted to rush to him, fling her arms around him, seek and find his lips, be swept away by passion and make exquisite love in front of the warm fire. She didn't want to think. She only wanted Blue.

But she didn't move.

She would be hiding, she knew, in a haze of blissful ecstasy, losing herself in the beauty of lovemaking with Blue. She wouldn't have to deal with anything but the awe and wonder of joining her body with his.

But that wouldn't be fair. Not to Blue. Not to herself.

Blue turned from the fire.

"There's something you need to know," he said, his voice slightly gritty. "Since you're going to be thinking everything through, it's only right that you have all the facts."

Amy looked at him intently.

"Amy...Amy, I...I love you," he said quietly. "I am very deeply in love with you. It's forever love, I swear it is, and I'm...asking you to be my wife, my partner, the mother of my children. I want to share every Texas dawn yet to come with you. Amy Madison, I'm asking you to marry me."

"Oh, dear heaven," she said, tears spilling onto her pale cheeks. She pressed trembling fingertips to her lips for a moment, striving for control that remained beyond her reach. "I...no...I...I can't..."

"Shh." Blue raised one hand. "Don't answer now. Just think about it as you're doing your sifting and sorting. Know that I love you with all that I am, and will always love you. Believe that, Amy, as you work through your confusion.

"Think about living here on the Rocking B, watching our children grow up, hearing their laughter and ours filling this house to overflowing. This house would become a home if we were married. *Our* home. Ours."

"Oh, Blue," Amy said, sobbing. "Don't say any more, please, please, don't." She got to her feet, praying her legs would support her. "I have to... I must... Good night, Blue." She hurried from the room.

Blue watched her go, a knot in his gut, an ache in his throat.

"Good night, my love," he said to the very empty room.

Shortly after dawn the next morning, Amy folded the last sheet she'd stripped off the bed and placed it on top of the neat pile of linens. She looked around the bedroom for something, anything, to delay leaving the safe haven of the room.

Sighing in defeat from not finding further busywork, she juggled the suitcase, computer, purse and the tote bag of books and left the room. Depositing her cargo at the front door, she stood quietly for a moment, reaching deep within herself for the courage to face Blue.

She was exhausted. She'd hardly slept the previous night because she had been unable to quiet her raging thoughts. Around and around in her mind, the circle of confusion had spun, bouncing from one dilemma to the next with increasing, tormenting speed.

And echoing over and over was Blue's voice, along with the vivid, magnificent image of him standing in the glow of the fire and Christmas lights.

I love you with all that I am, and will always love you.... It's forever love.... I want to share every Texas dawn yet to come with you. Amy Madison, I'm asking you to marry me.

"Oh, dear heaven," Amy whispered, pressing her hands to her cheeks.

Tears were hovering close, she knew, and she hated that, despised the fact that she was liable to walk into the kitchen, see Blue and burst into tears of total despair, caused by the confusion she was attempting, and failing, to deal with.

She dropped her hands from her pale face and splayed them on her stomach, taking a deep breath in the process, then letting it out slowly. Lifting her chin to a determined tilt, she marched toward the kitchen. Breezing into the large room, she stopped dead in her tracks.

The kitchen was empty.

Moving forward tentatively, she peeked into the mud room.

Empty.

She turned to see a freshly brewed pot of coffee with a solitary mug sitting next to it, waiting for her to reach for her healing breakfast.

And there on the table were her car keys on top of a folded piece of paper. With hands trembling so badly the keys jingled when she lifted them, Amy picked up the paper and opened it.

Tears filled her eyes instantly, and a sob caught in her throat. There was only one line on the sheet in a handwriting as bold and strong and confident as the man who had written it.

The message said, "Remember that I love you, Amy," and it was signed simply, "Blue."

"Oh, God," Amy said, the tears now streaming down her face.

Feeling childish, frightened, vulnerable and so incredibly alone, she ran from the room.

She ran from the Rocking B Ranch, driving her car that now purred like a contented kitten.

She ran from Blue Bishop.

But where, she asked herself frantically, could she run from herself?

Blue sat in the saddle on his horse, hidden in a cove of trees beyond the side of the buildings, and watched Amy drive away in a cloud of dust.

His jaw was clenched so tightly that his teeth

ached, and his knuckles were white from the hard pressures of his hands gripping the saddle horn.

When the little car had long since disappeared from view and the dust had settled, Blue took a rough breath, only then realizing he had been hardly breathing.

He tore his eyes reluctantly from the driveway and swept his gaze over all of the Rocking B he could see from where he was.

For the first time since he'd bought the spread, achieving his lifelong dream, the ranch looked barren, desolate and empty.

And Blue Bishop knew he was a very lonely man.

He was a man in love, who had just watched the woman of his heart leave his home perhaps—dear Lord, no!—for the last time.

Blue narrowed his eyes, tugged his Stetson low on his forehead, then spun the horse around, urging the sleek animal into a gallop.

He would give Amy time and space, he thought as the horse thundered across the land. He would wait. But only for a while. Because, by damn, he was one of the Bishop boys, and he didn't give up without a fight.

Never had.

Never would.

Two days later, Amy slid into the booth across from her mother in a busy restaurant.

"I'm sorry I'm late, Mom," Amy said, catching

her breath. "I turned in my column on a week in the life of a Texas rancher, but the traffic between the *Holler* and here was horrendous."

"It's busy, all right," Margaret said, smiling. "Combine Christmas shoppers with office workers on their lunch hour, and you have a lot of people out and about. Decide what you want to eat, then we'll get caught up on news."

Margaret handed Amy a menu, then sat back in the booth to look at her as she scrutinized the wide variety of luncheon offerings.

Margaret Madison, at forty-six, appeared younger, and on more than one occasion, mother and daughter had been mistaken for sisters.

Margaret was the same height and weight as Amy, and had the delicate bone structure her daughter had inherited. But Amy had gotten her curly, dark hair from her father. Margaret's short hair was strawberry blond with a few strands of gray, and was naturally wavy.

Margaret Madison was an extremely attractive woman who turned men's heads when she entered a room, a fact she was oblivious to.

At the moment, Margaret's lovely features were settled into a frown as she stared at Amy. The frown remained in place as a waitress appeared, took their orders, then hurried away.

"All right, daughter mine," Margaret said. "Talk to me. You look like someone who needs a nap.

There are dark smudges beneath your eyes, and you're obviously exhausted. What's wrong?"

Amy shrugged, then grabbed her napkin, smoothing it onto her lap.

"I just haven't slept well for a couple of nights," she said, not meeting her mother's gaze. "It happens to everyone from time to time."

"I see," Margaret said, still looking at Amy intently. "How did your stay at the Bishop ranch go? Your short stay, I should say."

"Oh, well, I needed to cut it short," Amy said, now fiddling with her spoon. "I told you that Gibson McKinley wants two feature stories a month from me, instead of just one. I had all the data I needed from Blue Bishop." She sighed. "*More* than enough data for my muddled mind."

"You have a muddled mind?" Margaret said, raising her eyebrows.

"Oh! Well, gracious, Mother, you would *not* believe how many different ongoing chores are involved in running a ranch like Blue's. Why, there are oodles of things to do, just oodles. For example... Never mind. You can read my column and find out the scoop."

The waitress reappeared with a large tray.

"Two chef salads with house dressing," the woman said. "Two iced teas. A basket of hot rolls. There you are, ladies. Enjoy your lunch."

Amy and Margaret ate in silence for several

minutes, Margaret taking three bites of salad to Amy's one.

"Amy," Margaret said quietly, "do you want to talk about it?"

Amy looked up at her mother. "My salad? It's a big salad, very tasty and big."

"Nice try. You've been using that tactic since you were about six years old. It didn't work then, it doesn't work now. Sweetheart, I leave for Florida tomorrow morning. Christmas is a handful of days away. Do you expect me to go blissfully off knowing you're obviously distressed about something?"

"Yes," Amy said. "No. What I mean is, I was hoping you wouldn't notice I was...preoccupied."

"Silly girl, I'm your mother. I'm the last person on earth you should try to fool. So, do you want to talk about it?"

"I don't know. I'm so confused. Mom, let me ask you something."

"Certainly."

"Did you ever resent, even a little, the fact that you gave up a very promising musical career to be a wife and mother?"

"No, I didn't. Even if I hadn't met and married your father, I don't think I would have lasted long as a concert pianist. All that traveling... No, I'm too much of a homebody."

"Oh."

"But, Amy, women don't necessarily have to give

up their careers when they marry. They combine their worlds.''

''Which is wrong,'' Amy said, leaning slightly forward to emphasize her point. ''Having a career, being a wife and being a mother are too many roles for one person. She won't excel or be the best she can be in *any* of them.''

''Yes, she will.''

Amy straightened. ''No, it's impossible.''

''My goodness, Amy, I had no idea you had such strong feelings on the subject.''

''Well, I do, and I have for a very long time. You *could* have had a brilliant career, Mother. You sacrificed it for Dad and me.''

''No, I didn't. I just explained that. The constant travel wouldn't have been my cup of tea, husband and baby, or no husband and baby.'' She paused. ''But the career possibility I had was rather unique. Let's talk about your average career woman...like you.''

''Me? Oh, well, yes, all right. Hypothetically, of course.''

Margaret took another bite of salad, chewed and swallowed.

''Of course,'' she said. ''Hypothetically. Eat your lunch.''

''I'm not very hungry,'' Amy said.

''No appetite. Not sleeping well,'' Margaret said. ''Interesting.''

''It's not interesting, Mother, it's ridiculous. I'm a

dedicated career woman. I know who I am and what I want. I know where I'm going and what it will take to get there. No one is going to pull me from my chosen path."

"So there," Margaret said, smiling. "Do you want to stamp your foot now? It would be a nice touch to your tantrum."

"Thanks a lot," Amy said, frowning. "Let's go back to 'hypothetically.' What makes you believe that a woman *can* have a career, be a wife and a mother and still manage to do an excellent job in every role?"

"It's simple, dear," Margaret said. "She has added one very important ingredient."

"Which is?"

"Love."

Amy blinked. "Pardon me?"

"Honey, when love is intertwined in all that a woman does, things fall so nicely into place. Oh, I'm not saying there won't be days that are disasters, when she feels overwhelmed by it all, but I'm talking about the big picture.

"Wife? Mother? Career woman? Of course she can do it all. You're tripping yourself up with your measuring stick of excellence, Amy."

"What do you mean?" Amy said, pushing her salad to one side.

"Maybe the pie she served for dessert came from the bakery, instead of her making it from scratch.

Maybe she has a service come in once a week to clean her house.''

"Ah ha!" Amy said, pointing a finger in the air. "She's having to cut corners, making do. Excellence is now kaput.''

"Is it? While she's paying someone to scrub her bathtub, she's holding her child on her lap for a story. The time she *didn't* spend making that pie, she met her husband for lunch, just the two of them.

"With the extra energy she has because she's not attempting to do it all, her career benefits, as well. She's not drained, physically, or emotionally. Oh, yes, my darling Amy, we women *can* have it all, if it's firmly set in a foundation of love.''

"Oh," Amy said, in a small voice. "Oh, damn, just what I didn't need. More data. Ohhh, I'm a wreck, a total mess, a confused, befuddled—''

"How's Blue Bishop?" Margaret interjected.

"I'm in love with him," Amy said. Her eyes widened, and the color drained from her face. "Did I just say 'love'?''

Margaret laughed softly, a lovely smile lighting up her face.

"You did, indeed, say you were in love with Mr. Blue Bishop of the Rocking B Ranch. I figured that out shortly after you sat down. I wondered when you were going to tell me. No, let me rephrase that. I wondered when you were going to admit it to *yourself.* Now then, how does Blue feel about *you?*''

"He...he said he loves me, wants to spend a lifetime of sharing Texas dawns with me. Blue...Blue asked me to marry him."

"Oh, Amy," Margaret said gently, "the man you love returns that love in kind, and wishes to spend the rest of his life with you. This is so wonderful, romantic, special. You should be floating on air, bursting with happiness."

"I'm not," Amy said miserably.

"That's quite obvious. You're confused. Darling, how can I help you?"

Amy sighed. "You can't. No one can. I have so much to think about, including everything you just added to the stack. Blue said he'd give me time to sift and sort. But how long will he wait?

"The Bishop brothers usually go after what they want. I can't picture Blue being patient for very long."

"I see. Amy, are you accepting the fact, deep within your heart, your soul, that you're in love with Blue?"

Amy nodded. "Yes. Yes, I love him. It happened very quickly, but I truly love that man with every breath in my body. I also know—" she swallowed past the ache of threatening tears in her throat. "—that I might very well have to walk away from Blue, that love, if I can't find an inner peace about marrying him, being his wife, still having my career. I need answers to so many questions."

"You'll discover what you need to know," Margaret said.

"Yes. I won't rest until I do. But Mother? I've believed for so very long that women must choose between a career and family.

"It's so important to me that I'm the best I can be at what I'm undertaking. I just don't see how I can be satisfied with my performance in that many roles."

"Well, when you have the answers you need, you'll know what to do. I'll be thinking of you while I'm away, believe me. I wish I wasn't leaving you right now."

"No, it's best. I really should be alone." Amy forced a smile. "Well, let's go Christmas shopping like we planned, shall we?"

"All right. But, Amy, when you sit down to think things through, look into your heart and ask yourself where you would wish yourself to be next year at this time.

"Do you want to spend all your future Christmases with Blue Bishop? Think about it, my darling daughter. Oh, do think about it."

Chapter Twelve

Gibson McKinley chuckled as he leaned back in the chair behind the desk in his office, the telephone cradled between his head and shoulder.

"Amy is on her way, even as we speak," he said. "She wasn't smiling, believe me, but she went. Nice guy that I am, I didn't ask her to salute before she stomped out of here... Yep, tomorrow she goes to phase two...No, I'm *not* her favorite person at the moment."

Gib moved forward as he listened, and began to doodle on the paper desk mat.

"You bet it will be worth it if this works. I'm with you one hundred percent... No thanks are necessary... Yes, I'll be looking forward to seeing you again, too. Keep me posted. Good luck, Blue."

* * *

Gibson McKinley was out of his tiny mind, Amy fumed as she weaved her way through the throng of people in the shopping mall.

Gibson McKinley was letting power go to his giant, economy-size head.

Gibson McKinley was becoming a very bossy boss, and for two cents she would punch him right in his handsome nose.

Amy stopped in her tracks as she took in the scene before her. An instant smile formed on her lips, a soft smile, a wistful, womanly, gentle smile.

Oh, look at that, she thought. Gib had sent her to gather facts for A Day In The Life Of Santa Claus feature. Not a week, just a day, due to Christmas being just around the corner.

And there was Santa. And on his lap was a little boy about four years old, speaking so seriously to the jolly old soul. What an enchanting picture they made.

Amy hurried forward and stood behind Santa's high-backed chair.

"I been good, really good," the youngster said to Santa Claus. "Cross my heart and stuff like that."

"I'm pleased to hear that you've been good," Santa said. "Have a candy cane. Are you putting out milk and cookies for me on Christmas Eve?"

"No, my daddy said you liked pizza better."

"Ho, ho, ho," Santa said. "That will be fine. Off you go now."

As the child was led back to his mother by a teenage girl dressed as an elf, Santa looked over his red-velvet-clad shoulder.

"Amy Madison?" he said. "From the *Holler?*"

"Yes," she said, smiling. "Just pretend I'm not here, Santa."

"What do you want for Christmas, Amy?"

Answers, she thought, inwardly sighing. A million, zillion answers.

"I'll give it serious thought," she said, "and get back to you."

"You'd better hurry, because there isn't much time left."

"Yes," she said quietly, I know."

"Ho, ho, ho," Santa bellowed. "Here comes my next customer."

There isn't much time left, Amy's mind echoed. Just how much time was Blue willing to give her? How long would he wait while she dealt with the maze of confusion in her poor, tired mind?

Blue Bishop. Dear heaven, she'd actually gone and fallen in love with Blue. And she missed him more than she would be able to put into words.

After leaving her mother's house last evening, she'd spent a restless, tossing-and-turning night. There was so much to deal with, so much.

And now, as if everything wasn't boggled enough, she knew she was in love with Blue. But what she didn't know was if she would ever tell Blue how she felt about him.

"Da-da."

Amy's attention was jolted back to where she was and what she was doing. She looked at the baby perched on Santa's lap.

The little girl appeared to be around a year old, and was dressed in red overalls and a red-and-white-striped shirt. She had dark, curly hair and big blue eyes.

Amy's breath caught as she stared at the baby, and a funny flutter tiptoed around her heart.

"Da-da," the baby said, clapping her hands. "Da-da. Hi, hi, hi."

"Hi to you, too, sweetheart," Santa said. "Merry Christmas and ho, ho, ho."

Santa gave the toddler a candy cane, and the elf carried the little one back to her mother.

Wait, Amy thought. She wanted to gaze at that beautiful child for a few more moments. Dark curls, big blue, *sapphire-colored* eyes... She and Blue might have a little child who looked something like that angel. It would be Blue who answered to the name Da-da. And she, Amy Madison, would be Mommy.

Oh, my, Amy mused, then sighed aloud. A baby. A child created from making love with Blue. A miracle, a gift so precious.

Stop it, she admonished herself. Her job was to gather facts for a column on how a shopping-mall Santa spent his day. She wasn't supposed to be daydreaming.

She would pay attention to what Santa Claus said

to the endless stream of children. She would listen to what the future leaders of the country were asking Santa to bring them as gifts in their youth.

Amy narrowed her eyes.

If Blue Bishop suddenly materialized before her right now, she would have an earful to deliver to him, she thought angrily.

How dare he say she might not want to be a wife and mother at all and was using her career as an excuse, *an excuse,* to avoid those roles?

The nerve of that man. He was so wrong, so off base, it was a crime. Blue was full of baloney.

Amy gazed at the two-year-old boy now on Santa Claus's lap.

He was adorable, she thought. Finally, she had an answer to at least one of the tower of questions plaguing her. There was no doubt in her mind that her maternal instincts were alive and well. She could check that off her dilemma list.

But still the question remained of how a woman could have a successful career and a happy family.

How could she have it all?

That night Amy had a strange dream about Santa Claus giving a baby with a bright bow on top of its head to her as a Christmas gift. Then another Santa entered the scene carrying a baby, then a dozen more marched in, each holding children of different ages.

It was understood in the dream that the little ones

were Amy's. It was also a given that she was ecstatic that they all belonged to her.

There was a sudden shift in the dream, and the smiling Santas became Blue Bishop still wearing the red-velvet outfits. He snapped his fingers, and a taller-than-he-was stack of white bakery boxes materialized instantly out of thin air.

Blue opened the cartons to reveal cakes, cookies and pies, and all the babies clapped their hands and cheered at the sight of the store-bought goodies.

She saw herself in an enormous kitchen, then Blue pointed to the boxes as he took her by the hand and led her from the room to join him and the children.

A stack of pajamas appeared out of nowhere, and together, she and Blue prepared the babies for bed.

Blue read from a huge storybook, then handed the volume to Amy to finish telling the tale to the wide-eyed little bundles. One by one, they tucked the babies into cribs, kissing each good night.

The dream jolted Amy awake before her alarm went off, and she sat bolt upward in bed.

Blue, and babies and bakery-bought desserts? she thought foggily. Blue had actually endorsed the treats made by someone other than herself, and the children had been pleased as punch.

A non-homemade pie had been one of the examples her mother had used to illustrate how needs could be met by simply doing things differently.

In the dream Blue had been right by her side, doing his share, caring for the babies with her, babies who had been obviously happy and contented.

There was something whispering at her, Amy realized, in the back of her still-sleepy, haven't-had-my-coffee-yet mind. What was it? What was that elusive whatever it was?

Wait, it was becoming clearer. Blue had said it and... Yes, there it was.

Compromise.

Amy pulled her knees up, wrapped her arms around them and rested her chin on top.

Compromise, her mind echoed. A career woman who wanted, needed, the fulfillment of having a husband and children had to compromise, had to learn what was really important in the overall scenario of her existence.

Did it really matter if treats were bought at the store or made from scratch?

No.

Did it matter who cleaned the house, or did the laundry, as long as the tasks were completed?

No.

Did it matter if groceries were ordered over the telephone, as long as the cupboards and refrigerator were stocked with nutritious food?

No.

"Oh, my," Amy said, her eyes widening.

If the end result was that everything on a list of what needed doing was somehow completed, wasn't that the mark of excellence?

Yes!

She smacked off the alarm before it rang. Leaving the bed, she stopped and surveyed her apartment.

It was a studio with a tiny alcove kitchen. Her bed took up the majority of the living area, with space left only for a nightstand, two small easy chairs, a television on a metal cart and a minuscule dining table with two wobbly chairs.

This was where Amy Madison, the career woman, lived. Any spare money went for the tools of her trade: a fancy portable computer and some day a printer.

There was no warmth here, no homey feeling. It was simply a few square feet where she ate, slept and worked, then walked away from each morning to devote herself to her career.

There was nothing in this place to give her a hug.

Amy turned slightly to see vivid colors creeping beneath the shade on the window. She crossed the floor and snapped up the shade, her breath catching as she drank in the sight of the spectacular, vibrantly colored Texas dawn.

I want to share every Texas dawn yet to come with you.

Blue's passionately spoken words hummed in her mind, over and over, as she gazed at the sky.

She turned again finally to look at her little apartment, wrapping her hands around her elbows.

This wasn't a home; it was four walls, a ceiling and a floor. It was sterile and cold.

Why hadn't she seen it for what it was before now?

Because before now, she hadn't been in love with Blue Bishop.

She'd changed and grown since meeting and falling in love with Blue. She now wanted more in her life than what she had had, because *she* was more than who she had been.

Amy sank onto the edge of the bed, her heart racing, knees trembling.

Was it possible? Was it really, *really* possible that she could have it all?

What about her journalistic career? True, she had done extremely well to earn her own feature column so quickly.

But what about the future? She wanted her name to be recognized, respected, her byline a guarantee to the readers that the story they were about to read would be compelling, the facts totally accurate. She wanted to achieve so much as a writer.

Did it matter who wrote her story, as long as her name was on it? she thought dryly. How could she compromise in the arena of her career?

"Oh, dear," she said, pressing her fingertips to her temples.

She'd been making fantastic strides in discovering a great many answers to the towers of questions tormenting her. But now she'd hit a brick wall, and confusion and despair were creeping in around her once again.

She glanced at the clock, then jumped to her feet.

Gib had been in a rush when he'd given her the Santa Claus assignment. He'd also handed her a piece of paper with a name and address on it.

She was to write another "A Day In The Life Of…" column, featuring the person whose name was on the paper. Gib had failed to tell her, however, what said subject did for a living.

"Great," she said, shuffling toward the kitchen to make coffee. "I'm really professionally prepared here, researched to the max." She shook her head. "Darn you, Gibson McKinley."

After consulting her trusty city map, Amy drove across town, giving the steering wheel several friendly pats as the car performed perfectly in the heavy traffic.

The address she was seeking proved to be a medium-size, two-story Colonial-style house in a quiet, pretty neighborhood.

Amy parked in the driveway and told herself not to frown. She would have to fake it, give no clue whatsoever to the person inside the house that Amy Madison, reporter extraordinaire, didn't have the foggiest idea who said subject was or what she did for a living.

If Gibson McKinley worked for her, Amy thought as she approached the front door of the house, she would definitely fire him.

Amy rang the bell, heard the lilting chimes echo within, and a moment later the door opened.

The pretty woman, who was smiling at her, appeared to be in her midtwenties, had blond hair caught up in a ponytail and was dressed in jeans, tennis shoes and a sweatshirt. She was cradling a cute, hefty baby boy on her hip.

"Hello," Amy said, matching the woman's smile. "I'm Amy Madison from the *Holler*."

"Come in," the woman said. "I'm Jessica Anderson. Well, you already know that, of course."

Of course, Amy thought dryly. Whoever heard of a journalist arriving to interview someone when they didn't know whom they were arriving to interview?

As Jessica closed the door behind Amy, she kissed the gurgling baby on the forehead.

"And this," Jessica said, "is Anthony. He's going down for his morning nap, due to the fact that he has been awake since the crack of dawn. Have a seat in the living room, and I'll be right back."

"Thank you."

Amy wandered into the living room and smiled as she saw the cluttered array of toys on the floor. The room was pleasant, homey, with furniture that was stylish but obviously meant to be used by a family, as evidenced by the sturdy green-and-blue-tweed upholstery.

"There we go," Jessica said, coming into the room. "Would you like some coffee?"

"No, thank you."

"This is going to be fun," Jessica said. "I was so tickled when Betsy called me and asked if I'd take part in this."

"Betsy?"

"Betsy McKinley. Well, she's not 'McKinley' anymore, but we grew up together and are very close friends. I still think of her as Betsy McKinley."

"Gibson McKinley's daughter?"

"Right. Didn't Mr. McKinley explain the connection to you?"

"It must have slipped his mind."

"Well, anyway, this is great. Just think, I'm going to be the subject of a column for the *Holler.*"

Why? Amy mentally yelled. What do you do all day?

"A Day In The Life Of A Work-At-Home Mother," Jessica went on. "That's me, all right."

Thank you for sharing, Amy thought.

"Shall we go into my office? I have a monitor in there so I can hear anything that's happening in Anthony's room. It saves me jumping up and down to check on him. If he even squeaks, I can hear him."

"That's very efficient," Amy said, taking the recorder from her purse.

As she followed Jessica from the living room and down a hallway, Amy spoke quietly into the recorder, relaying the discovered subject matter of the column and the information about the baby monitor.

The two women entered a large, sunny room. There was a drafting table near a sparkling bank of windows, a wall of filled bookcases, an easy chair, table and lamp and a playpen.

"This is where I work," Jessica said, gesturing around. "Anthony is willing to stay in his playpen for quite a while, because he can see me. He's only seven months old, though. Once he's toddling, I'll have to consider taking him to a sitter's for part of the day, or having someone come in to chase him while I'm busy."

"Mmm," Amy said.

Jessica crossed the room to the drafting table.

"As you know," she said, "I'm a free-lance artist. I've done mostly advertising work in the past years. But now? Oh, heavens, it's so exciting, my dream has actually come true."

"It has?" Amy said, trying to sneak a peek at the large paper spread on the table.

"Yes," Jessica said, her eyes sparkling. "I've signed a contract to do the illustrations for a children's book. It's a wonderful tale about a whole slew of perky little animals in the woods."

A funny fluttering sensation swirled in Amy's stomach, and she frowned slightly as Jessica chattered on about the story in the book.

A children's book? Amy thought. Jessica's dream had been to illustrate a children's book, while Amy's had been to *write* a book for children.

How had Gib known about…? No, no, that was ridiculous. It was merely a coincidence.

It was the same uncanny timing of Gib sending

her to do the Santa Claus column. The day with the endless stream of adorable children visiting Santa had settled, in the affirmative, the question of whether she wished to be a mother some day.

But Gibson McKinley wasn't capable of reading her mind, for Pete's sake.

"I have the very best of both worlds," Jessica said, bringing Amy back to attention. "I'm at home with my baby *and* pursuing my career goals. Even if Anthony goes to a sitter's for part of the day, I'll still have the comforting knowledge that I'm available if he needs me, no matter what."

"Yes, I can certainly see the advantages of your working here at home," Amy said. It was perfect, just absolutely perfect. Jessica was so fortunate. "It's marvelous."

"When I take a break to stretch a bit," Jessica said, "I toss in a load of wash, or call in a grocery order. My husband, Tony, picks up the groceries, dry cleaning, whatever, on the way home. He works for a corporate law firm.

"If Tony has to go out of town, the grocery store delivers, or Anthony and I go out together after his afternoon nap and do the errands."

"Perfect," Amy said. "I envy you, Jessica, I really do. I imagine a great many women who read my column about you will feel the same as I do."

Jessica cocked her head to one side and looked at Amy.

"Well, you won't need to envy me when you're

working at home as I do," she said, appearing rather confused. "Betsy McKinley said you were *very* seriously considering doing exactly that. She said you were going to write a column on a work-at-home mom, but your main purpose for coming to my house was to gather the nitty-gritty details of how it all goes."

Alarm bells went off in Amy's head, and a cold shiver whispered down her spine.

"Yes, of course," she said. "Now then, I'll just sit over there in that comfy chair and let you go about your normal routine. Pretend I'm not here."

"Okay," Jessica said, sliding onto the high stool behind the drafting table.

Amy's trembling legs managed to carry her to the easy chair, then she sank onto it gratefully, her mind whirling and her heart racing.

Her being at Jessica Anderson's was no coincidence, she realized. Spending the day with Santa Claus and the children was beginning to feel phony, too.

What on earth was going on here?

These two assignments had come directly from Gibson McKinley. Why was he seemingly determined to provide her with answers to questions regarding her relationship and her future?

Amy narrowed her eyes.

Blue Bishop.

Anger began to creep in, consuming Amy with ever-growing fury.

Blue Bishop was in cahoots with Gibson McKinley. Yes, it all made sense. Blue had done Gib a favor by allowing a reporter to take up residency at his ranch. Now it was payback time from Gib to Blue.

Blue was attempting to manipulate her, push her buttons, by having Gib send her on custom-ordered assignments.

Blue wasn't keeping his word one iota. He'd promised to give her time and space to sort and sift through the muddle in her mind.

Was he doing that? No.

Was he respecting her need to be alone to think? No.

Was he playing sneaky little games with her head when she was so very vulnerable, with Gib as his partner in crime? Oh, yes, that was exactly what was taking place.

She was going to strangle Blue with her bare hands.

She was going to weep buckets for a week and a day, because Blue wasn't the honorable, trustworthy man she'd believed him to be.

Like a spoiled child, Blue was determined to get what he wanted at any cost, not caring if he rode roughshod over her emotions.

Not caring if he broke his promises to her.

Not caring if his actions showed a painful lack of respect for her feelings, for her as a person, a woman.

Blue had betrayed her.

He had destroyed all they had together, and what they might yet have shared in the future.

She was so angry she could spit.

And she was so brokenhearted she felt as though the very essence of herself were crumbling into dust.

She would get through the long hours of this day...somehow, Amy silently vowed. Then she was heading out of town, straight for the Rocking B Ranch.

She was going to pay a visit to one Mr. Blue Bishop.

Chapter Thirteen

While Amy's car covered the miles to the Rocking B without one sputter or cough as she drove along the flat road, her emotions were having a roller-coaster trip.

From nearly one minute to the next, she was catapulted from fiery fury to dark despair, which resulted in her frowning one second, then sniffling the next.

There was a time, she knew, when Amy Madison would have done anything and everything possible to avoid an unpleasant and upsetting confrontation.

Well, not anymore. She had changed so much since that first drive along this road, a map next to her on the seat in order to locate the Rocking B Ranch, owned by a man named Blue Bishop.

She'd changed her views on a multitude of issues.

She'd changed her goals and dreams for the future to include wishing for a husband and babies.

Her heart had changed; too, allowing her to embrace love, fall in love with Blue.

Amy sniffled, snatched a tissue from her purse and dabbed at her nose.

Somehow, she vowed, she was going to confront Blue with what he had done without falling apart. No matter how magnificent he looked, or how badly she might want to fling herself into his arms to be kissed, held, caressed, she would stand tall and firmly in place.

She would confront Blue with his tacky game playing, his broken promises and betrayal, then say goodbye to him for all time.

"Ohhh, dear," Amy said aloud as tears filled her eyes.

No, she absolutely would *not* cry in front of Blue.

As Amy approached the Bar None, she slowed, finally pressing on the brake in front of the property next to Blue's.

The house was completely gone now, every scrap of debris having been hauled away, leaving a large section of glaring, bare dirt where the home had stood.

Amy stared at the nothingness of what had been. The emptiness before her, she decided glumly, represented what had happened to her. She'd traveled this road leading to the Rocking B, had had her world turned upside down by Blue and fallen in love for the first time in her life.

And now, just like the home filled with memories that had once stood on the land at the Bar None, everything new and rich and real in her life was gone, as though it had never been there at all.

Oh, yes, she was still in love with Blue. It would take a very long time to dim the exquisitely beautiful memories of what she had shared with him.

But the Blue Bishop she was about to encounter was a stranger, someone who wasn't remotely close to being a man she could love and trust, who respected her, her wishes and her needs.

No, she wouldn't cry when she confronted Blue with what he had done, because Amy Madison didn't display that kind of raw emotion before someone she didn't know.

With a sigh, she tore her gaze from the barren patch of land and continued on toward the Rocking B.

Blue left the barn and started slowly toward the house, wondering absently what he would fix himself for dinner.

The mere thought of the evening meal brought instant images of Amy into his mind's eye. He saw her moving comfortably around his kitchen, then sitting across from him at the table, smiling and laughing.

Lord, he missed Amy so much, loved her so damn much.

He spent the nights in restless slumber, if he managed to sleep at all. The bed was too big, too empty, without Amy nestled against him.

Everything reminded him of Amy and produced an ache of loneliness. The Christmas tree, the fire in the hearth, the piano he'd never had a chance to hear her play, the kitchen, the bedroom...hell, the entire house, the whole damn ranch, echoed Amy's name over and over in his exhausted brain.

How long could he go on like this?

How long would he have to wait to hear Amy's final decision regarding the hope, want and need he had to share his future with her?

When, if ever, would he hear Amy Madison say *I love you, Blue?*

Blue sighed and slowed his step, having no desire to enter the big, empty house, eat a solitary meal and spend the evening in restless pacing in front of the fire.

The silence of one was painful and deafening.

He'd been overcome by a sense of panic, of stark fear, at one point, felt chilled to the inner core of his being at the thought that Amy might walk out of his life forever.

A desperate man did desperate things.

He'd called Gibson McKinley, a man he really only knew by name and sterling reputation, and asked for his help. Gib McKinley was a hell of a fine guy, and had understood Blue's frantic frame of mind. He had agreed to execute the plan Blue had concocted regarding specialized assignments for Amy.

Had the Santa-Claus-with-cute-kids and the work-at-home-mother bit worked, even a little? He had no idea, not a clue.

Had he been wrong to go behind Amy's back, attempting to nudge her decisions in the direction he so deeply desired them to go? He didn't really know. Was everything really fair in love and war? He didn't know that, either.

All he knew was that he was in love with Amy Madison. It was a love that was natural and right, and real. Lives were at stake here: his, hers and those of children they might have together.

Oh, yeah, desperate men did, indeed, do desperate things.

Blue's attention was caught by a puff of dust in the distance.

Someone was driving toward the house, he realized. He couldn't yet see the vehicle, but it was coming closer.

Blue stopped dead in his tracks, his heart thundering to the point it was actually painful.

Amy!

It was Amy, his Amy. She'd come to the Rocking B, to him.

Amy was home!

Blue took off at a run, arriving at the front of the house just as Amy got out of her car.

And then he froze, halted his flight three feet in front of her.

The euphoria he'd felt as he ran, the image in his mind of sweeping Amy into his arms, holding her close, whispering her name, then kissing her... kissing her...kissing her...vanished in the chilling dread that swept over him as he saw her closed and angry expression.

"Amy?" he said.

He searched her face for even a hint of a smile, of warmth, but found none.

"Blue," she said, nodding slightly. "I'd like to speak to you."

"Yeah, okay, sure," he said, feeling a trickle of sweat run down his chest. "Come into the house."

"I think not. What I have to say won't take long," Amy said. It couldn't, she realized. Because her legs wouldn't support her for more than a few minutes. "I'll stand right here, thank you."

Blue nodded, every muscle in his body tensed.

"I'm aware," Amy said, praying her voice was steady, "of the shoddy conspiracy you put together with Gibson McKinley to send me on assignments for the paper that *you* decided might work to your advantage."

"Amy, listen, I—"

"Let me finish." Amy drew a steadying breath. "I trusted you, Blue, believed in you, believed that along with your declarations of love there was the proper respect for me, the woman, the person. I thought your promises were real, that you understood my need to have time to think about all the questions I was dealing with.''

''I did...I do understand. I—''

Amy raised one hand to silence him.

''Really?'' she said. ''There's no evidence of that, Blue. None. You turned right around and attempted to manipulate me when I was so very confused and vulnerable. Your word, your promises are worthless. You played games with my emotions, with me.''

''No, oh, no, Amy, I just—''

''I can't forgive you for that, Blue Bishop,'' she said, mentally damning the tears beginning to sting her eyes. ''You destroyed my trust in you, what we had, who I thought you were. You left me with nothing but broken dreams and a shattered heart.''

Tears spilled onto Amy's pale cheeks.

''Damn you, Blue, I fell in love with you! No, wait, I fell in love with who I *believed* you were.''

A sob caught in her throat.

''But now,'' Amy went on, ''but now I realize I didn't even know you, not really. If what you did by joining forces with Gib felt natural and right, then heaven help me, you are a total stranger.''

''Amy, let me explain. *Please.*''

''No, there's nothing more to be said. It's over, Blue, finished, done. Before we hardly had a chance to begin...it's over.''

Blue took a step toward her and began to extend one hand in her direction.

"No," she said, "don't touch me, don't...just don't."

Tears flowed unchecked down her face and along her neck. "Leave me alone, Blue. No more games. No more trying to manipulate me. No...more... anything. Just...goodbye."

Amy got into the car, slammed the door and started the engine. She spun the wheel around and sped off, covering Blue in a cloud of dust he wasn't even aware of.

He turned just enough to watch her go, disappear, vanish, from the ranch, from his land, from his life.

"Ah, Amy," he said, an echo of unshed tears in his voice.

Amy loved him. She'd just said that she loved him. He was so damn sorry for what he'd done, but she hadn't given him a chance to explain how desperate he had been. He hadn't meant to hurt her, make her cry, break her heart. *He loved her.*

"Amy?" he said aloud. "Dear God, I've lost my Amy."

Time lost meaning as Blue stood alone in front of the big, empty house, staring in the direction that Amy had gone as she'd left him...forever.

Amy hardly remembered driving home, but was totally drained when she entered her tiny apartment. Putting one foot in front of the other took full concentration and effort. She dropped her purse onto the floor, flung herself across the bed and wept.

Hours later, after crying, dozing, then crying some more until she had no more tears left to shed, she pushed herself wearily to her feet, painfully aware of a roaring headache.

Gibson McKinley wanted articles on a Santa Claus in a mall and a mother who worked at home? Well, fine, that was what he would get. First thing tomorrow morning, she would turn in the two pieces, handing them to Gib personally.

Along with her resignation from the *Houston Holler* newspaper.

No, she wasn't resigning her cushy spot at the *Holler* in a fit of temper because Gib had been Blue's despicable partner in crime.

She was leaving the newspaper because she was taking control of her life. *She* would determine her future. *She* would decide what she would do and when she would do it. Never again would she be manipulated or given orders.

And what she did, she would do alone.

Gibson McKinley smacked the piece of paper he held onto his desk and glowered at Amy, who sat in the chair opposite him.

"I won't accept this," he said.

"You have no choice," Amy retorted, matching his expression. "I quit."

"Why?"

"That's really none of your business, Gib. All you need to know is, I quit."

"Amy, look," he said, his expression and voice softening, "if it's because of the part I played in the plan that Blue—"

"Please," she interrupted. "I don't wish to discuss that. My resigning has nothing to do with that."

"Oh?" Gib said, raising his eyebrows. "Blue phoned and told me what your reaction was when you discovered what had been done. Betsy's friend, Jessica, didn't understand the need for secrecy, or maybe I didn't get that across to Betsy. Hell, I don't know."

"What *I* know," Amy said, "is that I don't wish to discuss it and that my leaving the paper is separate and apart from that disaster."

"Amy Madison," Gib said, nearly yelling, "do you have any idea how much Blue Bishop loves you?"

Amy narrowed her eyes, pursed her lips and stared at Gib. He sank back in his chair and shook his head.

"Women are so damn difficult to deal with," he said. "There's just no reasoning with you once you're in a mind-set. Man, what a mess." He sighed. "I'm placing you on leave of absence."

"You can't. I quit."

"I'm the boss, remember? If I say you're on leave instead of terminated, then that's how it is."

Amy got to her feet. "Suit yourself...sir. I'll go clean out my desk."

"Amy, this is Christmas Eve. Aren't you even going to stay for the party in the newsroom this afternoon.''

''I'm not in a party mood,'' she said quietly. ''I'll say goodbye to Sue Ann and the others, then…go.''

''Where? Go where? What are you going to do?''

Amy lifted her chin and met Gib's troubled gaze directly.

''I'm going to live my life with no interference or manipulation from outside forces, Mr. McKinley. I'm taking charge of my life. I'll answer only to myself, while living and working all by myself.''

''I see,'' Gib said, though he clearly wasn't pleased with her decision.

And since there was nothing further to say, Amy turned and left the office.

''Well, Mother,'' Amy said, clasping her hands at her waist, ''what do you think? It's quite a change, isn't it? We're only five days into the New Year and I'm officially established as a self-employed freelance writer, working at home, being my own boss. And in my spare time, I'm concentrating on writing a children's book.''

Margaret Madison nodded and walked farther into the center of Amy's apartment, taking in the changes her daughter was chattering about.

The big bed had been replaced with a daybed dotted with bright pillows. The television cart doubled as a nightstand, and the dining set was now a computer table, with a place mat at one end for eating meals. A folding screen covered the view of the tiny kitchen. Only one of the easy chairs remained.

"You've accomplished a great deal in a short time," Margaret said. "It looks lovely, yet very professional, honey."

"Good, that's good. I sold some things, bought others at a secondhand store. I have business cards now, too, that say, Amy Madison, Freelance Writer. Reasonable Rates, Reliable, References. Catchy, huh?"

"Indeed." Margaret sank onto the easy chair. "My head is still buzzing, Amy. I returned from Florida to discover that you've completely revamped your life-style."

"It was time," Amy said decisively. "Gib finally relented and gave me two assignments to cover for the *Holler*. He still won't put through my termination papers, though. He's a very stubborn person."

"Won't you miss the people and the hubbub of activity at the *Holler?*"

"I've met Sue Ann for lunch once already. I like working at home, Mother. It's very convenient, extremely efficient and definitely cost-effective. And who knows, maybe someday I'll actually see published and on the shelves in a store, a book for children that I've written.

"See how wonderful everything is? I'm my own boss. I'm able to support myself with my freelance assignments *and* at long last I'm pursuing my life-long dream of writing children's books.

"I've decided not to buy a printer now and will keep that money as my emergency fund. I can rent printer time at a computer store near here. I've covered all the nitty-gritties, every one."

"Mmm." Margaret studied her daughter for a long moment. "Amy, what about Blue?"

Amy sat down on the daybed and straightened a pillow that didn't need straightening.

"I told you. It's over between us. Blue wasn't who I thought he was. I trusted and believed in him and he— Mom, I don't want to go over the details again."

"Amy, let me have my say for five minutes, please. This gruesome crime of Blue's that destroyed your belief and trust in him is— Well, don't you think that perhaps you're being a bit judgmental?

"Honey, you told Blue you were confused, seeking answers to many questions. Blue Bishop is in love with you. Is it so terrible that he attempted to show you the answers to some of those questions? Isn't it possible that he was fighting for your future happiness together?"

Amy jumped to her feet. "I can't believe you're condoning what Blue did."

"I'm suggesting you try to see things from his side, as well as your own."

"Mother, trust, promises, respect for another persons's needs, are the same on both sides," Amy said.

"All right, dear, I won't say another word on the subject." Margaret paused, then got to her feet. "I must go. I have a cutie-pie guy of eight years old to meet, who is determined to learn how to play 'Twinkle, Twinkle, Little Star' on the piano.''

During the next two weeks, Amy was on the go to the point that she fell into an exhausted sleep at night within moments of her head touching the pillow.

She was out and about, calling on businesses of all types to let them know she was available for freelance writing assignments.

A travel agency commissioned an article on an upcoming cruise package they wanted to promote. Two large corporations hired her to pen pieces for their company newsletters, one about pension benefits, the other on a proposed day-care center within the building.

Gib McKinley telephoned to say that the response to A Day In The Life Of... was even more positive than the A Week In The Life Of... column. He assigned Amy to do a day in the life of a meter maid, and one on a parish priest.

She was so busy, Amy thought as she prepared for bed one night. Wasn't this great? Everything was going even better than she'd hoped. She'd fully expected a dry spell while she established herself in her new endeavor, but she'd had a steady flow of work from day one.

She'd been running all over Houston, zipping here, there, everywhere, then zooming home to plant her bottom in front of the computer and type her little heart out.

Of course, she needed to go the extra mile as she started her fledgling business. But that wasn't the only reason for her hyperactivity. She'd been doing everything imaginable to keep from having time to think about Blue Bishop.

Amy sighed.

Oh, how she missed Blue.

The image of him in her mind's eye was so clear, so real, she felt as though she could reach out eager hands to touch him. She could see those incredible blue eyes, his smile, hear his laughter, even savor his aroma of fresh air and soap.

And she could see the pain on Blue's face on that last day at the Rocking B.

Amy slipped between the sheets on the daybed, snapped off the lamp and stared into the darkness.

She would *not* lie in bed and dwell on Blue Bishop. What was done, was done. Her aching heart would ease in time. And surely she would eventually stop missing him so much. The memories of all they'd shared together would dim.

Two tears slid down the sides of Amy's face.

"Oh, Blue," she whispered, "why did it have to end this way? Why couldn't we have had it all?"

Amy finally slept, her slumber restless.

And in the morning, like every morning, she automatically awakened without the alarm being set, to savor the beauty of the miraculous Texas dawn.

"I never..."

Chapter Fourteen

Amy sank onto the chair in front of the fire in the hearth at her mother's home.

"Ohhh," Amy said, with a moan. "I'm stuffed. That was a delicious dinner, Mother."

"I'm glad you enjoyed it," Margaret said, settling onto a matching chair across from Amy. "You never did say what you ate on Christmas to celebrate the day."

"There you go again," Amy said, laughing, "sliding in a Christmas question."

"And there you go again, not answering."

Amy's smile disappeared completely. "Let's close the subject of Christmas past, shall we? It was a bit...well, gloomy for me." *Horrible* was closer to the mark. She'd been so alone and lonely, missing Blue so very much.

"All right, Amy," Margaret said, shaking her head. "The subject of Christmas is officially closed." She paused. "Now then, what did you say we're to call this business we're going to do this evening?"

"Brainstorming," Amy said, her eyes immediately sparkling. "I'm still plotting my children's book, and I've hit a glitch. Writers often get together and toss ideas around. It's called brainstorming."

Margaret smiled. "Have you noticed that I'm not a writer?"

"But you have a wonderful imagination. You used to tell me fabulous stories when I was little, making them up as you went along."

"That's true. So, let's brainstorm."

"Great." Amy wiggled farther into the soft, comfortable chair. "Okay. My main characters are nine-year-old kids, a boy and a girl, who are best friends. The girl, Patty, is being raised by a single dad. The boy, Sam, is being raised by a single mom."

"Check."

"Patty and Sam feel that their mom and dad are both lonely and need someone to love. So why not get their parents together? If everything goes as they plan, they could all be a family together."

Margaret nodded. "Check."

"I'll make it clear that these children aren't just doing this for themselves, but because they each love their single parent very much. But how can they have the parents meet each other? That's my glitch.''

"Why?'' Margaret asked.

"I was going to have Patty pretend she hurt her ankle while playing at Sam's house. She would wail her head off, cry and call for her daddy. It would be a ploy to get Sam's mother to call Patty's father and ask him to please come over.

"My problem is this, Mother. *I* know that the children have the purest, loving motives for the charade. True, Patty's phony injury is a lie of sorts, but the plan has been concocted on a foundation of love.''

"Go on,'' Margaret said, looking at Amy intently.

"As an adult, I can understand what is being done and why, but am I delivering a confusing message to children? You know, that it's all right to lie to accomplish a good deed. That worries me. I'm afraid an editor won't like my premise of—''

"Whoa,'' Margaret said, holding up one hand.

"Yes?''

"As an adult, you understand why the children are attempting to maneuver the parents into a place where they will find something wonderful? Find answers?''

"Yes, of course, I see the loving logic of what Patty and Sam are doing. But this is a book for children, and I'm concerned that—''

"Oh, Amy, Amy,'' Margaret said. "Darling, listen to yourself. Would you please stop for a minute and really *hear* what you're saying?''

Amy frowned. "What do you mean?"

"Amy Madison," Margaret said, leaning slightly toward her daughter, "Blue Bishop put together a plan with Gibson McKinley to get you where you might be able to find answers to some of the questions that were tormenting you.

"The Santa Claus in the mall with all the adorable children, the mother who worked at home and had a career and a family. I sincerely believe that Blue acted out of the same kind of love that your Patty and Sam are.

"Amy, why aren't you capable of understanding Blue's motives in real life, as you claim to understand your fictional Patty and Sam's reasoning?"

Amy's eyes widened, and the sudden racing tempo of her heart echoed in her ears.

"Dear heaven," Amy whispered. "I... Oh, my gosh... I... What have I done?"

Margaret sank back in her chair. "Finally." She glanced heavenward for a second, then looked at Amy again. "After all these weeks, I hope you're realizing how terribly wrong you've been in your harsh judgment of what Blue did. What Blue did out of love for you."

Amy pressed trembling fingertips to her lips and nodded, unable to speak as tears closed her throat.

"And now?" Margaret said.

Amy dropped her hands heavily into her lap.

"I wish I knew how to give my subconscious a hug. The story I was writing was a message from the inner me, telling me how wrong I was, what terrible mistakes I've made.

"But, oh, Mom, what if I'm too late?" she said, her voice ringing with tears. "It's all so clear to me now. I was so hateful to Blue. Oh, Mother, what if he won't forgive me? What if I'm just too late in coming to my senses?"

"Well, I'd say there's only one way to find out, my darling."

"Yes," Amy said, getting to her feet. "I must go. I have to think this through." She gave her mother a quick hug. "Thank you so much. You have a dunce for a daughter. Oh, thank you, Mother." She hurried from the room.

"So that," Margaret said to no one, "is brainstorming."

She turned to gaze into the crackling fire, a lovely smile on her lips.

Early the next evening, Amy sat in a booth in a small café. The occupants of the seat opposite her were not going unnoticed by the waitresses on duty.

"Bram, Tux," Amy said, "thank you so much for agreeing to meet me here."

"Our pleasure," Tux said. "We only hope the subject matter is Blue."

"Whose name," Bram interjected, "fits his frame of mind, by the way."

"Yes, I *do* want to talk to you about Blue," Amy said. "I've been so foolish, so terribly wrong." She paused. "I have to ask you this. Is Blue involved with another woman now?"

"Are you kidding?" Bram said. "Amy, when the Bishop boys fall in love, it's forever. I'm still waiting my turn to find forever love, but Tux can verify what I'm saying. Blue is trying to figure out how to get from one day to the next without the woman he loves. And that happens to be you."

"I hurt him so much, and I'm so sorry," Amy said softly. "I'm hoping, praying, that he'll forgive me for what I did, what I said. I could go to him on my own, pour out my heart to him, but—"

"But?" the brothers said in unison, leaning toward her.

"I thought I could show my sincerity, my understanding, my belief in Blue, much better if I did to him what he did to me, all firmly grounded in a foundation of love. I do love him, more than I can begin to tell you."

"Dynamite," Tux said. "Where do Bram and I come into the picture?"

"Blue asked Gibson McKinley to help carry out a plan that Blue felt was the best thing for both of us. I viewed it as betrayal. To prove that I have finally come to my senses, I'm asking *your* help to carry out *my* plan."

Bram rubbed his hands together.

"Lay it on us, sweetheart," he said. "We're ready to roll."

"Amen to that," Tux said. "It'll be great to see Blue smile again."

"If this works," Amy said, sighing, "neither Blue nor I will be smiling if this plan doesn't accomplish what I'm hoping it will. Oh, Tux, Bram, I want to spend the rest of my life with Blue."

"Then let's leap into action," Bram said.

"What's the plan?" Tux said.

"Okay." Amy took a steadying breath. "Here it is. I want to turn back the clock and..."

Blue stopped halfway between the barn and the house. He shoved his Stetson up with one thumb and turned to stare at the barn, a perplexed expression on his face.

Chaps had just talked Blue's leg off. The old cowboy had rattled on and on, saying more than he had in the past three months total. It was as though he'd been bound and determined to keep Blue in the barn, for heaven only knew what reason.

Shaking his head in confusion, Blue continued on toward the house.

The whole day had been weird and frustrating, now that he thought about it.

Tink had come pounding on the door just after dawn to announce that cattle were loose in the north section.

Blue, Tink and Ricky had ridden out on horses to round up the strays. Once there, Tink had snapped his fingers, done a hokey gosh-and-gee-whiz routine and announced that he'd meant to say that cattle were loose on the far south corner of the spread.

Now it was dinnertime, and the entire day was shot. Three men had put three steers back where they belonged, using up the hours getting to the right place. Ricky had been amazingly calm about Tink's dumb behavior, while Blue had glowered continually at Tinker.

"Ah, hell, forget it," Blue said aloud.

A wasted day meant double chores tomorrow, but what difference did it make? One day was just like the next, so what the hell?

Crummy attitude, Bishop, he thought as he entered the mud room. Somehow he had to put Amy Madison behind him, push the memories of her into a dusty corner of his mind. He couldn't go on like this, operating by rote, having no enthusiasm for anything he was doing, tossing and turning through the long, lonely nights.

But oh, man, he missed Amy so damn much. He loved her. That love wasn't losing one iota of its intensity, wasn't dimming in the least as the weeks dragged slowly by.

Blue sighed, took off his boots and stuck his Stetson on a peg on the wall. He crossed the room, opened the door to the kitchen and stepped inside.

Blue stopped dead in his tracks.

Hell's fire, he thought. He'd gone and done it. He'd slipped over the edge. He'd lost his exhausted mind. Standing there in the big, empty kitchen, he could swear he smelled chicken cooking, just the way it had when Amy was at the Rocking B.

So, this was insanity, he thought dismally. His life without Amy was so barren, so lonely, he couldn't exist in its reality. His beleaguered brain had hurled him back in time to when he'd been with the woman he loved.

They would come for him now, haul him away to the funny farm, where he would live out his days as a blithering idiot who smelled nonexistent chicken cooking, prepared by an imaginary woman.

Blue shuffled forward slowly, only to halt again as he saw a piece of paper on the table. He peered at it cautiously, seeing the feminine-appearing writing. The message said, "Come to the family room. Please."

Not a chance, he thought. He wasn't following orders written on a paper that wasn't really there.

Or was it?

Reaching out one hand, he tentatively touched the paper, then snatched it up.

Nuts or not, he knew when he was holding a sheet of paper, damn it.

In the next instant, he strode to the stove and yanked open the oven door.

Cancel crazy, his mind hammered. There was definitely a chicken, surrounded by vegetables, baking in a pan inside that oven.

What in the hell was going on here?

He smacked the paper onto the counter and headed for the family room, his strides long and heavy.

In the doorway to the room, he stopped yet again, so abruptly this time that he staggered on his sock-clad feet.

There was a fire crackling in the hearth in warming welcome. In its traditional spot by the window was a fully decorated Christmas tree, the colored lights combining with the fire's glow to cast a rainbow hue over the room.

And standing next to the Christmas tree, wearing a full-length, red-velvet caftan, was Amy Madison.

"Amy?" Blue said, hearing the strange squeaky sound of his own voice.

"Hello, Blue," Amy said softly. "Merry Christmas."

"Merry... What? It's closer to Valentine Day." Blue shook his head. "Yep, I've lost it. It's true, after all. You're not really here. Merry Christmas?"

"You haven't lost your mind. I'm turning back the clock, Blue, to before I destroyed us and what we had together. I'm hoping you'll forgive me and let us have another chance."

Blue opened his mouth, realized he had no air in his lungs and snapped his mouth closed again. He started toward Amy, his wildly beating heart echoing its racing tempo in his ears. He stopped in front of her and drew one thumb gently across the silky softness of her cheek.

"You're real," he said incredulously. His eyes

flickered over the Christmas tree, the presents beneath, the fire in the hearth. He met Amy's gaze again. "You did all this? And the chicken?"

"With help. Blue, please sit down."

"Yeah, sure thing. Sure."

He moved to the sofa and sank onto it heavily. Amy walked to the edge of the hearth and wrapped her hands around her elbows as she looked at Blue.

This was it, she thought. The rest of her life would be determined within the next few minutes. *Oh, please, Blue, listen to me with an open heart.*

Amy took a steadying breath, then let it out slowly.

"I love you, Blue," she said, then lifted her chin, "with all that I am, as a person, a woman."

"Ah, Amy, I—"

"Please, please," she said, "don't interrupt. There's so much I want, *need*, to say to you."

Blue nodded, his gaze riveted on the vision of loveliness standing before him.

"I know that the way I behaved, the things that I said, the last time I was here at the ranch, don't give evidence of my love for you. I was so wrong, so terribly unfair that day. I wouldn't even listen to a single thing you were trying to say to me. Oh, Blue, I'm so sorry, so very, very sorry."

Every muscle in Blue's body was tensed to the point of pain as he forced himself to stay put on the sofa.

Amy was home. He wanted to leap to his feet, tell

her she didn't have to say another word. He'd heard
I'm sorry and he'd heard *I love you, Blue.* That was
all he needed.

Whoa, Bishop, he told himself. He had to respect
Amy's wishes and listen to everything she needed to
say.

Then he was going to take her into his arms. No,
he'd best keep his mind off that path for a bit, or he
wouldn't hear a word his lady, his love, was saying.

"When you conspired with Gibson McKinley,"
Amy said, snapping Blue back to attention, "I felt
betrayed, manipulated, as though you'd taken over
control of my emotions, my very life, to achieve *your*
goals.

"What I didn't give consideration to at all was that
what you did was for me, to hopefully help me find
answers to some of my questions. What you did was
for you *and* me, for us."

Blue nodded, but didn't speak.

"The Santa Claus in the mall with the babies, the
work-at-home mother... Oh, Blue, I did get answers.
Finally, I knew I wanted more than just a career. I
wanted a family. I wanted it all. Jessica even showed
me a way to make it work.

"But the man I'd fallen in love with, I truly believed, was not who I'd thought him to be. You were
gone. What we'd shared, everything, had vanished.

"I couldn't move past the chill, the disillusion-
ment of being convinced you'd betrayed me, hadn't
respected my needs. Oh, I was so wrong.

"I took what I'd learned from your plan made with Gib, and put it into operation. I quit my job at the *Holler* and started working at home, freelance."

Blue's eyes widened in surprise.

"I began to plot a children's book, pursuing my lost dream. It was when I was creating the actions of the characters in the book, plus the added ingredient of my mother's love and wisdom, that I came to my senses."

Amy glanced at the Christmas tree, then back to Blue.

"I could have just come to you, Blue, and asked you to forgive me for being so horrible, so quick to stand in harsh judgment of you.

"But I decided that if *I* concocted a plan with the help of others, did out of love what *you'd* done out of love for me, you'd truly be able to see that I understand.

"I wanted to turn back the clock to when we were so happy together. I wanted to celebrate the Christmas we didn't have. So I asked Tux and Bram to help me."

"My brothers were in on this?" Blue asked, his eyebrows shooting up.

"Yes, and they brought Chaps, Tink and Ricky into the operation. I believe your day was a bit unusual?"

"I'll be damned," Blue said, chuckling. "I'm surprised my mother wasn't part of the cast."

"She was. I drove by your parents' house, and she

handed me the roasting pan with the chicken and vegetables. I didn't have time to do more than prepare this room the way I wanted it.

"Tux cut the tree from your property in the dead of night, while Bram was whispering to Chaps about needing you away from the house all day."

"Unreal," Blue said, grinning.

"I manipulated you and maneuvered you to where I needed you to be...all out of love, just as you did for me.

"Blue, I'm begging for your forgiveness for how I reacted. I'm asking you to put that behind us so we can move forward. I want to be your wife, the mother of your children."

Tears filled Amy's eyes.

"Blue Bishop," she said, a sob catching in her throat, "will you marry me? Please?"

That did it.

There was no way that Blue could continue to sit silently on the sofa for one second longer. He lunged to his feet, took a long stride to close the distance between them and flung his arms around her, pulling her tightly to him.

"Blue," Amy gasped in shock, "I—"

"Wait," he said. "Now it's my turn. But what I have to say won't take long, because if I don't kiss you pretty damn quick, I'll probably die from going too long without kissing you."

"Oh," Amy said, staring up at him.

"Yes, I forgive you for pitching a fit all those

weeks ago. Yes, I understand how you felt. Yes, I think what you did here today with your sneaky crew was a loving display of what you now know to be the truth.

"And, oh, yes, Amy Madison, I'll marry you, have babies with you, share years of Texas dawns with you, *have it all.* I love you so much, Amy. I never stopped loving you, never will."

Tears slid down Amy's cheeks.

"Forever love," she said, smiling through her tears.

"Forever love," Blue repeated, lowering his head toward hers. "And, Amy?" He brushed his lips over hers. "Merry Christmas." Then his mouth claimed hers in a searing kiss.

A shirt and jeans, a cloud of red velvet and sundry other pieces of clothing were soon scattered on the sofa and floor as Amy and Blue sank onto the carpet in front of the fire in the hearth.

They held fast to each other, caressed, whispered endearments and, as each kiss fell on soft, feminine skin, and taut, tanned, masculine skin, a wound was healed, the pain forgotten, the days of the past lonely weeks erased one by one, kiss by kiss.

Passion soared. Hearts beat as one as bodies meshed into one, because they *were* one, united in love, for all time, forever.

They'd traveled a rough and rocky road to find their dreams, but they'd won the battle against doubts and fears.

Amy and Blue were home, on the Rocking B Ranch.

They made love, dozed, made love again, talked quietly of wedding plans and which room in the house should be Amy's office. They wondered absently if the chicken in the oven had turned to charcoal, and rejoiced in the fact that they were together again at last.

"Blue?" Amy said much, much later.

"Hmm?" he said, his eyes closed, one arm encircling her waist.

"Do you want to open the presents under the tree?"

"Can't move," he said.

"Shall I tell you what they are?"

"Good idea," he said. "You've worn me out, woman, but a man could die happy feeling the way I do right now."

Amy smiled. "Well, the presents are...one, a can of bug spray."

Blue laughed, then buried his face in Amy's fragrant curls.

"Two," Amy went on, "a canister set with pretty sunflowers on them for the kitchen."

"That's nice," he said, moving from her hair to one of her breasts.

"Ohhh, that feels so good. Where was I? Oh, the third gift is for later. It's a baby monitor like the one Jessica has, for when I'm working in my office here and the baby is in his room."

"*Her* room," Blue said. "I want a baby girl who looks like you."

"I want a baby boy who looks like you."

Blue's busy lips traveled to the flat plane of Amy's stomach.

"We'll have a couple of each," he said.

"Okay," she said dreamily as heated desire began to swirl within her once again.

Amy smiled and Blue chuckled, then no more words were spoken for a very long time.

Epilogue

"Glory be, isn't that just the most romantic thing you ever heard tell? For a spell of time, I was worryin' myself to a frazzle, thinkin' maybe Amy and Blue wouldn't get straightened 'round and get themselves back together. But it finally happened, and folks were might happy for 'em.

"They had their weddin' on the Rockin' B. I was there, you know, tappin' my toes to that country music, and eatin' enough to last my tummy for a week.

"Amy was a beautiful bride. And that Blue? My stars, he looked so handsome in his Western suit, so tall, strong, those blue eyes of his just shinin' with love for his Amy.

"Nancy and Tux were smilin'. Jana-John and Abe

were smilin'. Bram was smilin', but I knew he was wishin' he was in love, makin' plans for his forever. Well, as I told Bram, there's always a new day at dawn, and a person can't be knowin' what it might bring.

"Oh, and Amy's mother, Margaret, and that Gibson McKinley fella, who owns the *Holler*, sure did take to one another. They danced and danced, not seemin' to notice anyone else.

"Granny Bee, Bram said to me, look at that. Everyone is in couples, two by two. Bram, darlin', I said, pattin' his hand, your turn is comin'.

"Mark my words, Bram Bishop, your turn is comin'...."

* * * * *

Take 4 bestselling love stories FREE

Plus get a FREE surprise gift!

Special Limited-time Offer

Mail to Silhouette Reader Service™

3010 Walden Avenue
P.O. Box 1867
Buffalo, N.Y. 14240-1867

YES! Please send me 4 free Silhouette Special Edition® novels and my free surprise gift. Then send me 6 brand-new novels every month, which I will receive months before they appear in bookstores. Bill me at the low price of $3.34 each plus 25¢ delivery and applicable sales tax, if any.* That's the complete price and a savings of over 10% off the cover prices—quite a bargain! I understand that accepting the books and gift places me under no obligation ever to buy any books. I can always return a shipment and cancel at any time. Even if I never buy another book from Silhouette, the 4 free books and the surprise gift are mine to keep forever.

235 BPA A3UV

Name	(PLEASE PRINT)	
Address	Apt. No.	
City	State	Zip

This offer is limited to one order per household and not valid to present Silhouette Special Edition® subscribers. *Terms and prices are subject to change without notice. Sales tax applicable in N.Y.

USPED-696

©1990 Harlequin Enterprises Limited

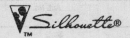

As seen on TV!

Free Gift Offer

With a Free Gift proof-of-purchase from any Silhouette® book, you can receive a beautiful cubic zirconia pendant.

This gorgeous marquise-shaped stone is a genuine cubic zirconia—accented by an 18" gold tone necklace.

(Approximate retail value $19.95)

Send for yours today...

compliments of ▼ *Silhouette*®

To receive your free gift, a cubic zirconia pendant, send us one original proof-of-purchase, photocopies not accepted, from the back of any Silhouette Romance™, Silhouette Desire®, Silhouette Special Edition®, Silhouette Intimate Moments® or Silhouette Yours Truly™ title available in February, March and April at your favorite retail outlet, together with the Free Gift Certificate, plus a check or money order for $1.65 U.S./$2.15 CAN. (do not send cash) to cover postage and handling, payable to Silhouette Free Gift Offer. We will send you the specified gift. Allow 6 to 8 weeks for delivery. Offer good until April 30, 1997 or while quantities last. Offer valid in the U.S. and Canada only.

Free Gift Certificate

Name: _____

Address: _____

City: _____ State/Province: _____ Zip/Postal Code: _____

Mail this certificate, one proof-of-purchase and a check or money order for postage and handling to: SILHOUETTE FREE GIFT OFFER 1997. In the U.S.: 3010 Walden Avenue, P.O. Box 9077, Buffalo NY 14269-9077. In Canada: P.O. Box 613, Fort Erie, Ontario L2Z 5X3.

FREE GIFT OFFER
084-KFD

ONE PROOF-OF-PURCHASE

To collect your fabulous FREE GIFT, a cubic zirconia pendant, you must include this original proof-of-purchase for each gift with the properly completed Free Gift Certificate.

084-KFD

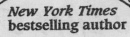

This summer, the legend continues in Jacobsville

Diana Palmer

A LONG, TALL TEXAN SUMMER

Three **BRAND-NEW** short stories

This summer, Silhouette brings readers a special collection for Diana Palmer's LONG, TALL TEXANS fans. Diana has rounded up three **BRAND-NEW** stories of love Texas-style, all set in Jacobsville, Texas. Featuring the men you've grown to love from this wonderful town, this collection is a must-have for all fans!

They grow 'em tall in the saddle in Texas—and they've got love and marriage on their minds!

Don't miss this collection of original Long, Tall Texans stories...available in June at your favorite retail outlet.

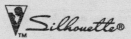

Silhouette®

And the Winner Is... You!

...when you pick up these great titles from our new promotion at your favorite retail outlet this June!

Diana Palmer
The Case of the Mesmerizing Boss

Betty Neels
The Convenient Wife

Annette Broadrick
Irresistible

Emma Darcy
A Wedding to Remember

Rachel Lee
Lost Warriors

Marie Ferrarella
Father Goose

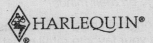 

ATWI397-R